Also by Ed Matthews

Harkers

Frontenac

Smithbury Skeleton

The Borax Boys

Sands Beach Aquarius

Bench Talk

Bench Talk

A Novel

Ed Matthews

SQUARE CIRCLE PRESS
VOORHEESVILLE, NEW YORK

Bench Talk

Published by
Square Circle Press LLC
www.squarecirclepress.com

Copyright © 2010 by Edward Matthews
All rights reserved. No part of this publication may be reproduced or transmitted in any form or by any means, electronic or mechanical, including photocopying, recording, taping, or any other information retrieval system, without permission in writing from the publisher.

First paperback edition 2010.

Printed and bound in the United States of America on acid-free, durable paper.

ISBN 13: 978-0-9789066-6-5
ISBN 10: 0-9789066-6-7
Library of Congress Control Number: 2010930908

Publisher's Acknowledgments
The cover design is by Conor Matthews and Richard Vang (Square Circle Press), using the Corel suite of graphics software. The text of this book was created and formatted by Square Circle Press using OpenOffice.org, a free suite of office software (www.openoffice.org). The title and chapter headings are set in Windsor BT, the text is set in Garamond.

Author's Acknowledgments
This is a work of fiction. Names, places, characters and incidents either are the product of the author's imagination or are used fictitiously, and any resemblance to any persons, living or dead, events or locales is entirely coincidental.

Bench Talk

Chapter 1

My name is Dave Foster and I claim Portland, Maine as my hometown. After high school I attended Potham College here in town before the Korean War interrupted my education. After my service time I returned to complete my undergraduate studies and then went off to the University of North Carolina to study and coach as a football graduate assistant.

Early in my first semester I met my future wife, Jane Rice. We got to really know each other while taking an advanced literature course, and by the end of our first academic year we ended our dream courtship by marrying in the university chapel.

After graduation we headed to Portland where I claimed my first adult job as an assistant football coach at my old school, Potham College. The next five years brought good fortune and change to our lifestyle. Jane was pregnant with our second child when we bought a comfortable house in South Portland that overlooked Casco Bay. Our run of good luck continued when I was named head coach at Potham. From that time on, our charmed marriage seemed too good to be true, but it was. Jane had gone from teaching English at Portland Central to a stay-at-home mom when Donnie, our second child was born. When Peggy, our youngest, reached middle school, Jane picked up her teaching career and continued in the classroom until retiring at the age of sixty-two, while I gave up work at sixty-seven. My coaching had been a satisfying success, once winning the Division III National Championship.

Retired life together was the very definition of happiness, which we savored every minute of the day.

This morning was more of the same but there seemed a different force around I couldn't account for. Being a creature of habit caused my routine to seldom change. I savored the solitude of silent moments before greeting a new day on my front porch.

The magic of the moment was to watch the sky take on hints of color, grudgingly give way to morning light, and finally blossom into a full-blown sunrise. After reading the *Cape Cod Times* while washing down several cups of coffee, the time was right to cross the street and claim my favorite bench that overlooked the majestic sight of Falmouth Heights and Vineyard Sound.

In a reflective mood after settling down, my thoughts drifted off to another time. I asked myself where my life would have headed if I hadn't retired from coaching. My days would probably have been full of what I did best, and not spent looking back to what-if situations of the past. But, every time I sit on my front porch, I'm reminded of the day my wife and I took possession of the house as our summer retreat. That precious moment represented a perfect time in our early marriage. It is often said that the only things you remember about the past are the good times. Well, don't believe everything you hear. I exhaled while trying to gather my senses.

Jane was the centerpiece of my existence until a massive heart attack claimed her life while we were eating lunch at a downtown restaurant. Jane was only sixty-three when she left me—far too young for such a vibrant woman.

Her passing left me in an unfamiliar veil of loneliness that is still with me. The last three years of my seventy-year old life have been in one gigantic holding pattern, all the time hoping tomorrow will be better than today, but continually entertaining doubts about that happening.

Nervous energy swept over me that couldn't be accounted for. My effort to shuffle through last night's dream and understand it failed, leaving me without a clue.

I felt the heat settling over the beach while staring at a near empty beach. The setting was right to start a new novel written by my favorite author, Justin Astor. His writing style captivated me mainly because his damn-the-torpedoes, straight-ahead stories centered on the sea with large doses of the military thrown in to attract readers to the evil and havoc he conjured up. Astor also wrote about Jack O'Brennan, a retired Bridgeton, Virginia detective who specialized in unsolved murders.

The saltwater smell reminded me that reading was the natural thing to do when enjoying the beach. A feeling of serenity swept over me as I gazed ahead, drinking in the scene that played out in front of me. Looking out across the placid waters of Vineyard Sound, I marveled at the clearly defined outline of Martha's Vineyard, the renowned playground of the wealthy, and destination of day-trippers from the Massachusetts mainland.

Yesterday the blue water displayed its unruly side of a mean sea with five-foot waves thumping against the beach. It was an untidy scene, to say the least, although today was different. Calm waters welcomed a handful of sailboats drifting across the relatively smooth surface. The Island Queen, a majestic ferry carrying day-trippers on its forty-minute trip to the Vineyard, caught my eye. Flags waving in the gentle breeze in front of seaside houses identified the occupants' native nationalities, favorite colleges, or organizations, a mishmash of personal preferences. Multi-colored beach umbrellas sheltering sun worshipers from cancer causing ultra-violet rays spotted the beach.

Gazing at water that sparkled under the sun's amber rays, I realized a warm day verging on torrid was in store, but days like this should be taken one at a time and enjoyed for the joy they bring. Falmouth Heights is what an ocean side retreat should be. To me, it means being in the company of family and friends in a relaxed retreat from the daily grind of life. Over-eating, getting sunburned, searching for shells and sea glass, fishing from the beach at night, and drinking a cold beer—what more could a man ask for?

A fine day to start a new adventure, I thought. Instead of a Jack O'Brennan mystery, I chose Justin Astor's latest novel, *Sunken Iceberg*. After starting my new read, I occasionally interrupted my concentration to survey the foot traffic that traveled the walk in front of me.

Moments after returning to my novel, I noticed a solidly built man dip his head in a nod as he effortlessly moved along in a smooth gait, all the while keeping his eyes on the walk as if looking for a crack that might upend him. Placing him around my age, I raised my hand in greeting and then returned to my reading. Half-an-hour later he returned along the sidewalk, stopping to silently stand in front of me. Even though deeply entrenched in Astor's novel, I sensed his presence. The stranger nervously rubbed his mouth before breaking the silence. He coughed and then asked, "Do you mind if I sit down?" The question was posed with the rich mellow tone of a Virginia accent.

I tried to ignore the interruption, but my unguarded solitude seemed shattered as I made a welcoming hand gesture, accompanying a chin nod.

"Not, at all." I think my smile made the newcomer feel welcome.

It was a defining moment in my life when our diverse histories came together on that bench; although at the time I didn't realize how his presence would dramatically redirect my life.

An awkward silence settled over the bench for several minutes before the new arrival moved to a more comfortable position. Intuition prompted me to introduce myself to the other man.

"By the way, my name is Dave Foster, and I'm from Portland, Maine." I extended my hand to the stranger whose handshake was brief but solid.

"It's good to meet you. I'm Charlie Jamison and Bridgeton, Virginia is where I'm from," he said with a soft-edged voice. He ran a hand over his gray brush-cut, his attention focused on the distant Vineyard nestled comfortably in the sound.

I was dazzled by the striking beauty of the area and hoped Jamison would leave as soon as possible. Reading was better than listening to some stranger who would probably make incessant banter of little interest to me.

At the same time a well-appointed woman near my age walked by, prompting me to consider what she might look like before stepping into her stylish athletic gear.

"Did you get a load of that?" he asked.

"Indeed I did," I replied. At least he liked what he saw, thus removing any doubt in my mind about how he viewed the opposite sex.

We sat quietly watching the activity that swirled around us until he spoke, a smile crossing his face.

"I feel like I can reach out and touch the Vineyard." After that, time passed as we sat in silence. Finally, Charlie picked up where he left off. "This whole area has a quality hard to describe. One can hardly look away from a setting like this," he said with conviction, heartily exhaling. "This breathtaking view kind of grows on you."

After hearing Charlie carry on about the scene I knew so well, my mind left his one-way conversation to retreat into my own thoughts, like a tortoise pulling into his shell. I could hear his words outside my head, but they had no meaning until his next sentence snapped me back to the present.

"Life at times is like running into a brick wall, and whatever is left is waiting to go wrong."

From time to time I had experienced moments of doom and gloom; his thoughts were not words I cared to hear on such a grand morning. I felt the need to redirect the conversation, so I asked: "Does your wife visit the beach?"

Jamison stiffened, a dark shadow settling on his face. An excruciating quiet passed before he slowly turned to face me. "Betty used to love the beach, but unfortunately she passed away two years ago."

I didn't know what to say, but I knew instinctively he was suffering. A number of questions flashed through my mind, however, it felt prudent to hold back and remain silent. I sensed his need for conversation emanated from deep grief that apparently consumed him. Strangely, I liked the manner in which he managed his distress. I couldn't help myself and asked: "Do you want to talk about it?"

By some unknown coincidence, two tired old men saddened by the loss of their wives found themselves living with questions they couldn't answer.

"Thank you for understanding. Times have been difficult for me of late, and perhaps you're the one I need to talk to. That will have to happen on another occasion, maybe tomorrow," he nodded in resignation.

I felt caught off guard by Charlie's startling revelation. He rose, reached for my hand, and then walked away toward the side street opposite the bench. He departed not with the vibrant stride he earlier displayed, but rather the slowed down pace of an emotionally distressed man. His departure left me with an empty feeling.

After Charlie left, I sat thinking about my new acquaintance's emotional state, understanding his sorrow, but nevertheless feeling helpless. Words alone couldn't aid him at this stage of his life.

The sun's scalding rays proved too much, forcing me to cross the street and settle on my front porch. Only a stone's throw from the beach, it proved much needed relief from the dog days of August. Charlie's mention of losing his wife began to register while I idly gazed at the water. Soon my memory took over, bringing my deceased wife's face into focus.

Chapter 2

It was just before seven when I settled on the bench, my novel tucked under my arm. I started to read when suddenly Charlie slipped down next to me. We greeted each other and then talked about baseball. When our enthusiasm waned, I redirected the conversation.

"How are you holding up?"

Charlie shuttered. "How can anyone understand my loss?"

I gave him a hard look. "They can't, so get over thinking they can. You've been having a difficult time since your wife passed away two years ago, but remember, life is for the living."

The look on his face indicated he wasn't happy with my observation. If he's not happy now, how will he react to what I had to say next? I wondered.

"There's no possible way for me to understand your loss, nor will I even presume to try. I believe anyone who has lost a loved one, close friend, someone they can relate to, feels a unique experience. Remember, there is no prescribed manner in dealing with grief. You're on your own, my friend."

Charlie shuffled his feet, crossing and uncrossing his legs. He turned to me and admitted grudgingly, "I believe you're right," his voice filled with emotion.

I noticed the tattoo with an anchor and U.S. Navy under it on his forearm. Now was an opportunity to distract him. "I see you were in the navy. It's just a guess, but you probably served in the Korean War."

"Right you are. I got this baby," he touched the anchor, now a drab gray from age, with his other hand. "One night I got full of beer and decided a tattoo was something I should have," he said laughing, a broad smile planted on his face.

He had a great laugh, and it was nice to hear him use it, I thought.

"I'd like to hear about your navy experience, any chance of that?"

Charlie started talking about his teenage years like a lead actor playing to a full house. His delivery flowed like a born storyteller.

"I joined the navy after graduating from high school in 1948. Following boot camp, I found myself in Underwater Demolition Training, a service I desperately wanted. My next sixteen weeks were spent in a living hell, wondering from day to day whether I was up to the challenge. Each new day brought another empty bunk in the barracks. The attrition rate was mind-boggling. The class that graduated looked like a skeleton cadre compared to what we started with.

"From South Carolina, the survivors moved to San Diego where advanced training followed. After finishing we had no idea where we'd start our frogman career. Our contingent found out in a hurry. Orders directed us to a small naval installation situated on the west coast of Kyushu Island, Japan. It was good duty. The fact we were frogmen weighed heavily in our favor, and provided us with an obvious insulation from the general military population."

Charlie paused to shift around to a more comfortable position.

"The worst part of the stint was dealing with our commanding officer. He was a hard charger of the first degree and worked us into a physical frenzy. That rascal worked on our mental toughness that brought me to a psychological fortitude I never realized before." Charlie shook his head in wonder. "My indoctrination to the real world of war came when North Korea crossed into South Korea with a lightning thrust that turned into a full-blown war.

"The next thing that happened came in a flash that forced me to experience the most dangerous moment of my young life. I found myself with a fellow frogman in a submarine heading for Wonson, the largest Communist naval base on the North Korean coast. Our assignment was to blow up a large transport resting in the heart of the harbor."

This is the stuff novels come from, I thought.

"At the time it seemed my main concern was to blow that ship up, but there was something else," he said with a wide smile. "I wanted to save my skin in the process."

Charlie paused to gather his thoughts.

"I can see it like it happened yesterday. The submarine settled on the bottom, roughly a mile out from the entrance of the harbor. After leaving the submerged sub through the escape hatch we were on our own. Using Munson Lungs, we quickly floated to the surface. The cold water shocked me even though we had trained in similar waters off Sasebo. So here we were, quietly swimming on the surface toward the center of the harbor. The unnerving part of the maneuver was observing the ambient light that shown in the imposed blackout and the routine noises emanating from our target. Viewing that ship as we approached, and knowing our assignment was to blow it up, seemed a daunting task. Suddenly we were alongside at mid-ships."

Listening to Charlie was like reading an action novel, I reminded myself, but he neglected mentioning how his commanding officer brought him to a physical frenzy.

"We checked our watches, and without a word spoken, swam off to our assigned mission. After finding my targeted area of the hull, I had a hell of a time locating a bare spot on the side because the barnacles had settled on the metal plates. The hull was so loaded with shells it took me a minute or so to attach my charge. After completing my assignment, I got out of there as fast as I could. We had set ten-minute fuses, so there wasn't much time to spare. I spent excruciating minutes at our meeting spot waiting for my partner. After he surfaced, we headed out to sea for our rendezvous with the waiting sub. It was pitch dark, but somehow the Koreans spotted us, maybe by the use of night-vision glasses, I don't know. The next thing I knew, we found ourselves under attack from small arms weaponry. I felt a pain in my left shoulder and immediately recognized I had been wounded. The injury was not what I expected, but rather like a bee sting if anything else. Harry, my partner, suffered a thigh wound that made it impossible to use his leg. So here we were in the middle of a pickle. Grabbing him by the cowling under his hood, I started a one-armed stroke, and swam like hell to get out of the firing umbrella. The explosion soon came, causing the ship to sink like a stone."

This story is long but interesting I thought while shifting my position on the bench.

"It was an hour later of swimming and pulling before I reached the surfaced sub with Harry. After getting us aboard, the boat immediately dove and headed for Sasebo. A corpsman checked me out and discovered I had a minor wound that barely raised the skin on my shoulder. Upon arriving at out base, my partner was taken to the infirmary, and later transferred to Yokosuka Naval Hospital on the mainland.

"I, on the other hand, confronted a different fate. Ordered to the operations officer, I gave him a complete report of our mission. Top brass had reaffirmed what I knew to be true. Apparently our charges had been properly placed and we realized a successful mission. Can you imagine those silly bastards telling me we had sunk a ship when I saw it go down in all colors of the rainbow?"

"That's something to be proud of," I offered.

Charlie merely shrugged.

"In the meantime, North Korean forces had driven down the peninsula in a sweeping operation designed to capture Pusan and its large naval base at the tip of South Korea. To counter the ferocious attack, Army and Marine Corps units set up an umbrella defense that ringed the city on the north. The unit I was assigned to in Sasebo was placed in the harbor area to deter attacks on our ships. Things didn't work out the way they sometimes do in combat. To this day, I don't know how it happened, but I became separated from my outfit and ended up with a Marine company on the perimeter. Instead of doing what I was trained to do, underwater demolition, I ended up playing Marine, fighting like hell to get through the day. I wasn't up front two days before I got wounded again."

His tale was so bizarre I couldn't help but laugh, prompting Charlie to join in.

"It sounds funny now, but it certainly got my attention back then. A random bullet knocked my helmet off, somehow leaving a slight groove in my scalp." He pointed to a pencil-thin scar that showed through the short hair over his ear.

"It sounds like you were really lucky."

"Indeed. But about that time I started having thoughts about how much luck was left for me. I was taken to an aid station where they treated the wound by placing a small battle dressing on it and then returned me to the front lines. For the reminder of day, I suffered the mother of headaches. After ten days of intense fighting, we managed to repel the enemy and send them packing up north. From there I reconnected with my unit in the harbor, and then was flown to Sasebo. Back again, I reported to operations and told my story to some commander, and the horse's ass just laughed! Maybe my experience sounded funny in Sasebo, but in Korea I didn't see much humor in it."

His wonderfully humorous comment sent me into a laughing jag. He looked at me until I motioned him to continue.

"I was assigned to a new unit in the morning, and later learned they would be an intricate part of an amphibious landing that would descend on the west coast at a place called Inchon. Three weeks after helping sink a ship in Wonson Harbor and stopping off to fight with the Marines, I had become involved in an operation I knew nothing about. Shades of Hollywood you may suggest, but about that time I found little entertainment in being a frogman.

"Douglas MacArthur, the UN Commander of the Korean theater, devised a strategy that would call for a sudden strike from the sea twenty miles west of Seoul. North Korean forces that formerly threatened to chase our forces into the sea now found themselves in a hasty retreat to their homeland. The thrust of the invasion was designed to cut them off before they safely reached the north. My unit was assigned to clear the beach where the planned landing would take place. Much of our assignment involved clearing mines. There's little doubt the Koreans anticipated the upcoming invasion. When they observed my unit on the beach, they started peppering us with mortar fire. After completing our work we headed out to meet with our landing craft. While under water I felt a pain in my hand. I had no idea what caused it, but sensed I had been wounded. After surfacing, the cause of the pain became evident." Charlie raised his left hand minus the tip of the index finger.

"The dirty sons of bitches had shot me again. After reporting to sick bay, I was told my wound wouldn't require surgery. So, here I was with three wounds and figuring on a trip home, but that's not the way it happened. I returned to Sasebo for the next several months where I trained hard in the freezing Yellow Sea. We ran five miles a day with full shoulder pack, ate good food, and drank stateside beer. My group stayed in guarded anticipation of what lie ahead, but looking back, conditions weren't too bad. The honeymoon was over the day we were outfitted with cold weather gear.

"We ended up in the north. Our assignment was to knock out the bridges crossing the Yalu River into China. Suddenly the Chinese swarmed into North Korea, trapping us with our pants down. They literally chased us to the sea. During that retreat, a mortar exploded in back of me, peppering my ass and legs with shrapnel. After completing our withdrawal, I was transferred to a hospital ship where remedial surgery took place. The surgeon who worked on me indicated further surgery would be needed stateside.

"Finally, I was headed home, knowing full well the horrors of Korea wouldn't be revisited, certainly by me. My parents met me at National Airport in D.C. and drove me home to Bridgeton. Fortunately, a naval hospital was located in town. It took three operations to remove all the shrapnel. When they finished, my ass looked like a flock of woodpeckers had attacked me."

His loose, meandering description of his wounds caused me to laugh. "I don't mean to laugh at your misfortune, but it's funny in a sad way."

"You're right, Dave. I can laugh at it now, but at the time it wasn't much fun."

"Did your wounds cause problems later?"

"There was a ton of tissue damage, but nothing earth-shattering. So, no, I never experienced problems, thank God. I will say I had two good things happen because of my hospital stay. The Navy gave me a month of recovery time, and the big one, I met Betty, my future wife, who was a navy nurse at the time."

"That's some story," I said."

"It is that. I'm meeting an old college friend of mine for lunch, so I have to leave. It was good talking to you."

Charlie Jamison walked away without saying another word.

What a way to end a conversation, I thought. He just up and left, saying, 'It was good talking to you.'

Chapter 3

Yesterday, Charlie talked about his Korean War experiences, but I sensed he needed to be drawn into a situation where he would divulge the turmoil he suffered through his wife's illness. I thought about how to be sensitive about talking about his loss and arrived at no reasonable answer. The solution finally materialized after considerable thought. I would ask him point-blank about his wife's demise, and let him take it from there.

Why am I so driven to learn more about his wife's losing battle with cancer? I thought to myself. Presumably, it's a case of misery loves company. If that's the way it works, maybe this developing relationship with Charlie will trigger a return to painful thoughts of Jane.

As I look back, I felt Charlie understood my concern, and steeled himself for the bad memories he would talk about. I asked him the question he needed to hear.

"The happy times rolled by until three years ago when Betty was diagnosed with breast cancer. Somehow, I missed the reality that cancer doesn't discriminate when choosing its victims." Charlie swallowed hard. "It felt like I had been kicked in the head when I heard the key report. The news put me in the crosshairs of doubt; the doubt of how well she would physically tolerate her treatment, and how I would adjust to knowing her life was in serious danger.

"I tried to block that thought from my mind, but all the time felt something dying inside me." A grave look settled on his face. "I fought hard to take this all in, but it proved to be a no-win situation for me." His jaw dropped depressingly low while his shoulders sagged in surrender.

I wanted to say something comforting, but reasoned there was little I could say that would make Charlie feel better.

"Dave, I'll never forget the anxiety I felt the morning I accompanied Betty to her first treatment. Her eyes looked like those of a deer caught in a car's headlights. She was seeking a reprieve and had no place to go but the room at the end of the hall.

"She put on a brave front, but when we approached the treatment door I could feel her tense up. When the dreaded words "Oncology Room" came into view, Betty stopped in her tracks. It was like she wanted to turn around, but my gentle push on her arm persuaded her to enter.

"Upon entering, the room was not what I expected. It was more like a tea party that had gone out of control. The front desk was located in the middle of the room. I'd say eight lounge chairs were placed against the wall with small tables next to each, and chairs provided for those accompanying the patients. The receptionist processed Betty, leading her through the procedures that would follow on her maiden visit. She led us to some chairs, a soft one for Betty, a straight one for me. I observed the patients in various stages of receiving treatment, each one fighting a battle against an unseen adversary while harboring dreams of what could be. It was one of the longest moments I ever experienced in my life, and Betty told me later she felt the same way.

"Several minutes later, a no-nonsense oncology nurse approached and introduced herself as Dorothy. She began to explain what was in store for my wife. My first reaction to Betty's nurse was a negative one. To put it bluntly, I couldn't stand her and thought how unfortunate for Betty to have drawn such a mean person."

A young couple walked past us arguing, apparently not caring who heard them.

"Life's too short to be fighting on such a lovely day," I observed. After speaking, I immediately knew my comment wasn't appropriate for the moment, but pushed on. "I'm sorry for interrupting. You were talking about the oncology nurse."

"Dorothy explained to us that each patient received a customized regimen designed by their personal oncologist. It was at that moment a revelation swept over me: the woman I didn't like was to become my trusted and learned friend, and had dedicated her professional career to improve the quality of life for people suffering like my wife. Maybe she couldn't control Betty's spirit, but from the way Dorothy talked, she was going to try like hell to not let it slip away. This lovely woman whom I had totally mis-judged carried with her a passion to help beat away this horrible disease that had silently invaded her patient."

"You're right, my friend. The world is full of compassionate people who, like Dorothy, fight and claw through life with a goal foremost in their mind, and that is to uplift their fellow humans beings and give them hope," I said assuredly.

Charlie nodded in agreement. The strange look on his face in-dicated he had unleashed his emotions about losing Betty, and was determined to talk about them.

"She warned about the possible loss of hair, weight, and ap-petite, plus nausea that could follow. Dorothy also mentioned how cold objects from a refrigerator might bother her, and sug-gested Betty should wear cotton gloves to guard against the change in temperature.

"I took copious notes during her arduous five hour treat-ment. After leaving the hospital, she seemed to grow sicker on the twenty-minute ride home. After settling down for the even-ing, waves of nausea consumed her for hours to come. Strangely, after a restless night, she would wake up as her old self. Betty's energy level returned to what it was before she became ill. It didn't last long, waning in the afternoon as she became visibly worn out. By the third day she seemed totally listless and depleted of energy."

Charlie crossed and uncrossed his legs while wringing his hands together as if they were frostbitten. He was under a great deal of stress and it showed.

He picked up where he left off. "The next day Betty appeared stronger, and from then until we returned for her second round of treatment, she seemed uplifted and ready to face the second assault of medicine. I saw each new day as a fresh start for her. As the days passed, I felt myself becoming a co-victim of cancer and the chemotherapy treatment she received. Every two weeks we visited the infusion room. Betty received five hours of therapy while looking into the eye of death. The only uplifting moments of those depressing visits was when the nurses and support staff greeted us with a smile and spirit-building words. They provided her with a security blanket and, I must say, there wasn't an alarmist in the group. I sat next to her while the silent drip, drip, drip of the medicine methodically disappeared into her vein. As her treatments wore on, I found it more difficult to control my emotions with each passing day.

"During this difficult stretch, I prided myself on being a man of vision and hope while blindly assuming I could wish her through this terrible illness. Dave, the worst part of this ordeal was the guilt that came every time I looked at her. Then one day while eating her meager breakfast, she looked at me with a sickly smile, and said, 'Charlie, have a good life and please watch over the children.' I could feel my mouth drop, and at that moment realized there was no way she would recover. Betty would never give in to anything, but in that instance, she had surrendered to the inevitable 'Big Sleep' that stalked her since she got sick. Her declaration ignited my hidden emotions, and I cried like a baby."

The man next to me had lost complete control of his emotions and began crying uncontrollably. He probably didn't realize people were casting puzzled glances in his direction. After hearing his devastating account of losing his wife, he had every reason in the world to allow his emotions to flow. Some may view crying in public as weak, but Charlie was grieving for someone he dearly loved and owed an apology to no one.

Charlie exhaled heavily. "She died three days later, almost six months following her diagnosis. Betty made me feel sixteen one minute, a little crazy the next. That's how I remember her," he said with a smile.

Something clicked in my mind. Given the history of our brief friendship, I chose rather to listen, not talk, but the inevitable happened. A question raced through my mind that begged to be asked, so I asked it.

"Charlie, how did your children handle their mother's illness?"

"They were a tremendous help to me from start to finish, and since then, as a matter of fact. Dave, I have to head out. Talking about Betty's death has been a little too difficult for me, but thank you for listening. I hope to see you in the morning."

"Drop in early so we can have a cup of coffee on the porch."

He nodded in agreement, and then headed down the walk, leaving me to my reading.

I need to forget his emotional account of his wife's death; after all, he's not the only man to lose a woman he loved. If I continue to listen to him, his story will emotionally trouble me, I reminded myself.

Chapter 4

Old habits abound, and this was never more evident than on my porch. Reading has always been an important part of my life. One might call it a quirk, but I never look at the back dust cover that contains the story description, author's bio, and picture.

After rousing from my mid-afternoon nap, I reached to the floor for the book I had been reading when I nodded off. Much to my astonishment, Charlie Jamison looked back at me. A brief bio nestled next to his picture informed me of the author's name —Justin Astor. Charlie was traveling under an assumed name. My favorite author's secret was out, at least with me.

The next day after going through my early morning routine, I settled on my bench thirty minutes earlier than usual, anxious to talk with Charlie about his latest novel and the pseudonym he had so brilliantly hidden.

Half an hour later he sat down, nodding his greetings to me. "Here's the coffee I promised," I said while pouring from a thermos. "How are you this morning?"

"I'm feeling better after seeing you. Thank you for remembering the coffee."

"I've got something that may interest you." I handed him his recent book face down. "We have something in common, but with one big difference. You write these great stories while I read them. Meeting you is a complete surprise and a genuine treat. I'm puzzled though as to how to address you. Is it Justin Astor or Charlie Jamison?"

He smiled at me shyly. "Just call me Charlie Jamison."

Intrigued by his answer, I asked, "This is none of my business, but why use a pen name?"

He didn't speak for a moment, and then answered. "As I look back, by the time I finished my first novel, *Hot Water, Cold Water,* which didn't get published by the way, I had pretty well decided on another name. That's how Justin Astor came about."

"You still didn't tell me why the change," I reminded him.

He smiled modestly. "No, I guess I didn't." Charlie tilted his head to one side, seemingly the natural thing for him to do when searching for an answer. His gentle manner made it easier to wait for a reply.

"I wanted a demarcation between my married life and professional career. It was a simple answer to a complicated question. Even before my first novel was published, my instincts told me I'd be a successful writer. There was no need to involve Betty in the life I was about to choose. I believe the average man develops a fierce spirit while fighting through the quagmire called adult life." He moved his shoulders in a shrug accompanied by a happy laugh. It was a sincere gesture, one that was appealing.

"Your novels are terrific regardless of what name you stamp on them."

"Thank you, Dave, that's nice to hear. We're two ordinary guys who came together by accident. My friends call me Charlie; I'd like you to do the same. I'm Justin in my mind, and on my books, that's all."

"Your style has a way of sneaking up on a reader. How do you write such marvelous stories?"

A heavy set man with a massive stomach waddled by, laboring with each step.

"That's a belly only a Buddha could love," Charlie remarked. His observation was more off-handed than mean-spirited.

Our conversation started to rundown when a harried woman with three youngsters passed by, two riding bicycles, the other with an old-fashioned scooter. Something about that scooter brought me back to when I was five.

"Did you have a scooter when you were a kid, Charlie?" I asked.

A slight nod provided his answer.

"It was sixty-five years ago when I came downstairs and spotted a bright red scooter under the Christmas tree, much like the one that kid has. I almost wet my pants with excitement."

"That's good, maybe I can use it someday."

"Here's something else that may interest you. The kid across the street from where I lived in Casler was my age and best friend. Eddie and I rode our scooters constantly all around the neighborhood. Those old scooters had a platform to put your foot on. In back was a curved brake blade that when pushed with your other foot rested against the tire and stopped it. At some point the hard rubber came off the rear wheel, but that didn't stop Eddie. Without the tire the brake hardly worked, so he took it off and used his heel."

Knowing full well where I was going, Charlie laughed.

"You guessed it. When Eddie stopped, the y shaped rim's two edges ground into his heel. Pretty soon the heel had more grooves than rubber. That didn't bother Eddie, but when his dad noticed, he went crazy."

Charlie smiled but didn't comment.

"Here's something you may remember. During the Depression many men fixed their family's footwear by placing the shoe on a last, and then nailing new heels they bought at the Five and Ten on them. Still angry, his father fixed the brake and then replaced the beat-up heel with new ones, half an inch wider than the old ones. With the heel sticking out wider than the shoe, the curious repair didn't bother Eddie in the least, but everyone else laughed their asses off."

"I'll hold on to that. Old guys our age will get a kick out of it," Charlie pointed out.

"Getting back to your writing, I'm curious about how you put a novel together."

Charlie thought about my question. "Let's start with my method. Writers may have a different approach to how they shaped their story. In my case, think of a tree. My storyline is the trunk. The roots are the major support parts of what I'm building, and that's where the fun begins. A writer has the latitude of allowing these parts to grow where they take him—within reason that is. Lesser parts of the story are the smaller branches. You must remember that anything added to this story must have a structural discipline that maintains the integrity of the story.

"Dave, this isn't working for me. I'm going to take this in another direction. You've read all my books so you'll understand where this is leading. Somewhere along my writing career I needed a change. There's a Bridgeton cop known as the "Tracer of Unsolved Murders;" his name is Jack O'Brennan, a remarkable man who once headed the detective division. He's the central figure in my mystery novels. After deciding to change genres and write a detective mystery, I read back issues of the paper and came up with a beauty. Do you remember *Frontenac?* That was his case.

"We met for the first time and got on well. I told him what I had in mind, and he readily agreed to talk about the case. If you recall, it was about a guy named Harry Stafford who lost his job and had the misfortune of losing his wife and two small children in a freak motor vehicle accident in downtown Pittsburgh both on the same day. Born in the same city of German immigrants, he felt there was nothing left for him there. With that in mind, Stafford migrated to Heidelberg, Germany where he observed the rise of Hitler and his Nazi Party. He didn't like what he saw in the Fatherland and met with American officials about becoming an undercover agent.

He returned to the states and settled in Boston, a hotbed of German clandestine activity. He infiltrated the German-American Bund and passed information to the FBI. Our hero was discovered and directed by the FBI to leave Boston and relocated to Upstate New York under an assumed name.

He settled in a small village at the north end of Cayuga Lake and quickly established himself in a new life with a local woman. Nazi agents tracked him down and killed him, dropping him in the lake while heavily weighted down. That's the end of our hero. Do you recall anything about my story?"

"Yes, I remember feeling bummed out about him being killed."

"You know, Dave, truth is sometimes stranger than fiction. In the Frontenac incident, what I'm about to tell you is the truth. O'Brennan had an aged uncle living in the small village of Union Springs. He received a call that told of the old man's death. Being the only remaining relative, he traveled to New York to oversee funeral arrangements. About the same time he arrived, an intriguing event occurred. A skeleton washed up on Frontenac Island, a tiny island a quarter of a mile off the village shore." A smile crossed Charlie's face. "You know where I'm taking this."

"I think I do. If I recall correctly, the skeleton turned out to be the man killed by the Nazis."

"Bingo. Jack finally discovered the history of his existence in Union Springs. That left me with a good story, but no lead in or finish. I realized research had to take place, but where to begin? Understanding much of the story's impact occurred around Cayuga Lake, I needed background information about the area. Thus a trip to Union Springs was needed. I organized my thoughts, but came up empty on too many unknown facts.

"In my business, a helpful thought sometimes revealed something that may possibly bring a new sheen to the surface. The thought of an old Navy friend, Art Henry, came to mind. I had kept in touch with him over the years and we would occasionally get together. It seems he came from Central New York, but I didn't know where. He moved to a Pittsburgh suburb after his service time, so I gave him a call. We carried on as old friends do until I told him of the Frontenac incident. Art interrupted, telling me he was raised in the area. In fact, he went to high school in Union Springs. Art invited me to Pittsburgh for a visit and I readily accepted. That's the moment luck entered the life of this storyteller.

"I spent three days at his home and had one hell of a time. Dave sent me on my way with pages of names, localities, and the general landscape of the area. As a matter of fact, he lived in Cayuga, a tiny village at the north end of the forty-mile-long Cayuga Lake. He mentioned the location of his home which I put in the novel."

"That's amazing how you happened onto that nugget of information," I suggested.

"It is." Charlie appeared to think for a minute. "I'll tell you a funny story when I was up there. One morning he suggested we go out for a beer at his VFW home. Arriving at the club, we discovered it was closed and wouldn't open until noon. After banging on the door for awhile, the bartender opened up and invited us in. She had been setting up the bar when we interrupted her work. Art introduced me to her, and there we sat, drinking Iron City Light. Minutes later a buzzer sounded, allowing a middle-aged woman to enter. She settled at the bar, then spoke to Dave and nodded to me.

"He waved at her as he spoke. 'Good morning, Isabelle. Have a beer on me. I'd like you to meet an old friend from my high school days, Father Charlie Jamison.' Her eyes bright, she raised her glass in a thank-you gesture, outwardly appearing to preen. I sensed a foolish spell was about to descend on us, and my navy friend had brought me there. Feeling embarrassed by his comment, I quickly recovered. "Isabelle, it's nice to meet you and hear your voice.

"Art rolled his eyes at my greeting and said 'You're some piece of work,' he said, whispering out the side of his mouth. As we were leaving, I felt compelled to finish our brief beer fest with a final comment.

"Isabelle, maintain a good thought. I'll keep you in my prayers and pray that God is with you." I directed the sign of the cross at her while departing. Imagine this, Dave, all done by a good Protestant.

"My three days with Art had presented me with a different light on the subject of two obscure villages from the eyes of an insider. The four days that followed my trek from Pittsburgh to the Frontenac area caused me to sense something unusual was in the offering. It also provided me with a different take on where I planned to take the story. That's the way it sometimes happens."

Charlie stood up, made a stretching motion, and walked away, calling over his shoulder, "Well, it was nice talking to you, and maybe we'll meet again."

I watched my new friend walk down Worcester Court. He just up and left with no warning. Charlie was an interesting guy with a friendly personality, but a little on the peculiar side, I reflected.

Chapter 5

After telling me 'maybe we'll meet again' yesterday, Charlie was back at the same stand acting as if his abrupt departure hadn't happened.

He started our morning talk by asking questions about my experience growing up in a small town. It was at that time I sensed he was building a stockpile of incidental tidbits that he might use in a future novel.

If that were the case, I decided to do all I could to help him. When he asked me what incident or personality from my youth stood out; I was taken by surprise. It took several minutes to reach back in my Casler vault of memories for something he could use.

"My memory goes back to the first day of sixth grade. I remember a little girl, Catherine Hislop was her name. She first got my attention when I noticed her standing in the doorway of my classroom, shifting uncomfortably from one foot to the other. She carried distinct Scandinavian features, you know: blonde hair and light complexion. That morning had been difficult for her because the color was drained from her face, giving her a ghost-like appearance. She was wearing beat-up shoes, no socks, and a threadbare dress that couldn't hide the ravages of constant washing. That dress seemed to emphasize her gaunt demeanor." The memory of that poor kid prompted me to pause for a deep breath.

"Charlie, the thing I most remember is she had some kind of twine instead of laces in her shoes. Students looked at the newcomer without saying a word, immediately recognizing her situation."

Charlie grimaced through clenched teeth. "That's rough."

"Mrs. Warner, our sixth grade teacher, walked to the open door where Catherine stood, and took the admission slip she was holding. Back then, classrooms were equipped with old-fashioned desks that seated two students. Directing her to an empty seat next to me, she announced 'Class, this is Catherine Hislop.' Snickers of ridicule flowed through the room at the unsightly girl. That moment was early adolescence at its lowest point."

My new friend shook his head in disgust, motioning me to continue.

"The moment that little girl entered the classroom was a special time in my young life and helped shape the person sitting next to you. I can feel my shoulders sag in utter despair thinking about that bad time. Think about it, Charlie, that poor little thing was living a life that nobody knew about."

Charlie shifted around on the bench seeking a more comfortable position. "Dave, I hate stories like this, but it's important that I hear the rest. One had to experience that period to understand it."

"Isn't that the truth?" I responded. "The Depression had caused many families to lose their way through a minefield of hard knocks. I believe people our age felt the severity of those times in varying degrees. Some are marked for life, but nothing like the scars Catherine bore—her pain was immediately apparent."

"That's a sad story, but how could you remember it so vividly?"

"One doesn't forget images like I just described. Every time a teacher wasn't around, my classmates made fun of her with sly remarks and cheap lousy tricks. To make matters worse, there was a girl in fifth grade named Claire Franklin who led the verbal assault against Catherine. Any time we were away from the classroom and Mrs. Warner, Claire attacked her with spiteful remarks.

"She beat back this loathing by seemingly disappearing into herself for moments on end. The sign of her frustration would surface, followed by torrents of tears washing down her face."

"Dave, I'd like to store away your recollection of Catherine for safe keeping, and use it in a future novel, if I may?"

"I'd like that." The thought crossed my mind that the mention of a future novel sounded encouraging. Maybe the veil of funk he was carrying over his wife's death was lifting.

"Is there more to tell?"

I nodded but didn't speak. I felt recalling parts of a past long forgotten were a senseless effort. Suddenly the recesses of my mind opened and long-forgotten images of Catherine slowly returned.

"During that time I became curious about her past, but she displayed an unwillingness to reveal anything. The thing I most remember is thinking situations like hers should be resolved by grown-ups. Why do kids have to muddle through unpleasant circumstances they don't understand?

"My concern for Catherine wasn't lost on her. I remember one occasion when I stood up for her. She asked in a whisper loaded with despair, 'Why are you so nice to me?'

Her question forced me to take time before answering, I was that stunned. Finally I said, 'Because you're my friend and I love you,' came out much to my astonishment."

Charlie laughed. "Whoa! What happened then?"

I replied with a slight smile. "She didn't speak until school was dismissed. At that time I felt her tiny hand touch my arm. Catherine said with gentle grace, 'I'll never forget you.' I don't know how or why it happened in this moment, but she reached up and kissed me full on the mouth, and then walked away. I became a little unhinged and wanted to say something, but it was the same old story, I didn't know what words to use, so I remained silent."

"That's one hell of a story," Charlie said with a smile, "anything else to add?"

"There is. The next day she wasn't in school and never returned. Regretfully, she was out of the picture and we never said goodbye. I heard later that the Hislop family lived in a shabby part of town. Back in those days, families came and left run-down neighborhoods like the one in Casler for any number of reasons. I guess the Hislops were just such a family."

Charlie shook his head through a chuckle. "Mercy, love at first sight. That's pretty mature goings-on for a sixth grader."

His reaction caused me to laugh. "What the hell, I was twelve years old. What did I know about love?"

"Just remember, I'm always in the market for sketches of people like your Catherine."

I thought before speaking. "There's one more thing that just crossed my mind. I can't believe I neglected to mention such a tragic incident, but that's the story of my life of late. From the first day in school, I noticed Catherine's legs were covered with boils. Most were small, but some were the size of a quarter. She had a larger one on the outside of her right calf. Her legs was so thin, it really stood out. The boil was distended and roughly the size of a half-dollar. Back then it seemed massive to my way of thinking. It was awful to see her walking around with that ugly sore."

Charlie's eyes displayed discomfort.

"One day, Mrs. Warner called Catherine to her desk. When she pulled away to rise, her leg hit our desk, causing the massive boil to rupture. Yellow pus flowed down her leg into her shoe. To me, the tragedy of the occurrence was that she walked up to Mrs. Warner's desk without missing a beat. I thought at the time she had steeled herself to misfortune and this little incident was nothing more than another bump in the road."

Charlie appeared stunned, choosing not to speak. Silence claimed the bench while we sat grimly studying the water. After a considerable time he spoke up.

"It took a lot of courage for Catherine to face what lie ahead of her. She must have turned into some kind of woman."

I nodded in agreement.

"Dave, I get the feeling there's more to this story than how the kids in your school treated her. You're seventy years-old and still remember her like she appeared in your life yesterday. Why do I want to call this indelible impression you've recalled of a classmate more than unusual?"

Charlie's question caused me to draw a blank. Several minutes passed before my mind rebounded from his query.

"I really can't spell it out. She was pathetic looking, no doubt about it. You know the ugly boils on her legs, the nasty looking shoes, the worn-out dress that served as a shroud to cover her undernourished body. I'm at a loss explaining Catherine. Guess it would have to include all of the above, and maybe because she was so smart. No one with brains like hers should live such a life."

"After your tale about Catherine, I feel there's no wind in my sails. Dave, what do you say we walk to the corner and get a cold glass of beer? While we're at it, would you tell me about this Franklin girl?"

"That sounds like a sensible thing to do," I approvingly said, "and yes, I'll talk about Claire."

Chapter 6

"Why are you so interested in Catherine?" I asked while settling on a bar stool.

"It's not Catherine that interests me, but rather how she and other unfortunates managed to survive the Depression. After all, collecting insignificant facts that can be used later is what I do for a living. Maybe your portrait of Catherine needs writing about. Have you thought of that?"

"I haven't," I sheepishly replied.

Charlie smiled. "When you talked about Catherine I got the impression you had a crush on her and still carry a subconscious infatuation."

"Your assumption is completely off target. That said, let's drink some beer. The first beer always tastes the best," I observed.

Charlie nodded in agreement. "Now that we've got the beer thing out of the way, let's hear about Claire Franklin."

"Here's how it started. When I was in eighth grade, a seventh grader caught my attention. Much of my time in junior high was spent thinking how great it would be if she were my girlfriend, but that's as far as it went. When I was a junior, Casler won the regional basketball championship for the first time in school history. Our fans went crazy when the game ended and rushed the court to celebrate with the players. Suddenly a cheerleader hugged and kissed me. You guessed it, Claire Franklin was the cheerleader. She's the one you're interested in. At that point in my young life I became a pawn in her hands. From that moment on, we started a romance that continued during the spring. My dream had come true."

"Dave, would you describe Claire's physical appearance?"

"Why do you want to know about someone I can hardly remember?"

"That's what writers do. We store information that can be used later."

"Describe her physical appearance, you ask?"

His request didn't make much sense, but if it made him happy, why not cook something up? Minutes drifted by before I came up with an image that might satisfy him.

"Claire was tall, perhaps five ten and built like Esther Williams, the movie star. No artist could do her justice. She was a stunner, the best looking girl in school. Her eyes sparkled in bright sunlight like she put some magic drops in them. There is one thing I can still remember. Claire had such beautiful teeth; they'd be suitable for a Pepsodent toothpaste commercial."

Look at the way he's staring at me, I thought, he can't get enough. I might as well make her out to be a teenage queen.

"She had thick, shiny, brown hair that was incredibly luscious. Back then, she wore it long, but gradually shortened it as she grew older. As an adult, I'm certain her hair would've been spectacular. Claire had the best looking legs you'd ever hope to see, and when wearing heels, she'd stop traffic."

After finishing my narrative of Claire's physical attributes, Charlie looked delighted as if living in a dream sequence turning roses. He asked me to continue, a broad grin settling on his face.

"Claire kind of grew on me, and I liked the fact she was my girlfriend." I shook my head in disbelief and laughed. "That girl meant more to me than just a pretty face. My infatuation with her became so evident, my friends made fun of me. I remember thinking to hell with them. I was the one dating a dream, yet strangely, our relationship was not as I expected."

"What were you expecting?" Charlie asked excitedly.

"I never got to understand what she thought about things."

Charlie laughed at me. "You're an educated man, yet you sound like a fourth grader talking. What things? Tell me what you mean."

"I'm embarrassed to say the thought never entered my mind before."

I took my time before arriving at a reasonable answer.

"Claire liked music, but never played in the orchestra or mentioned a favorite band or singer. She wore nice clothes and always looked great but seemed to take her appearance for granted.

Learning was easy for her, but she never seemed to take an interest in any of her courses."

Charlie signaled with his hand for more about Claire.

"I'm certain she liked me for a time but never told me so. I know this analogy is stupid, but it's the best I can do. Imagine a white, puffy cloud floating by, constantly changing shapes before your eyes. Here one minute, gone the next. Claire was much like that cloud, always on the move, drifting. I remember thinking she was searching for something Casler couldn't provide. I had no idea what that something was, nor do I to this day. Maybe it was above and beyond my understanding of what drove her."

"Dave, I feel a head-turning story on the way." Charlie laughed. "Am I right?"

"Absolutely on target, but you're the writer, not me. Make what you want out of it."

He motioned me to continue with an enthusiasm I'd not seen before.

"On the last day of classes, high school students traditionally participated in a greatly anticipated event called "Moving-up Day." The special day started with homeroom attendance and then the students moved to the auditorium where each class was seated together. The freshman in the rear with the upperclassmen ahead of them and the seniors sat in the front rows. Sports letters, organization awards, and academic honors were passed out. Next, the seniors moved up on stage, followed by the lower classes taking empty seats ahead of them. It was a fun event. We were then dismissed to return to our homerooms to pick up our yearbooks. Following that, students were loaded on buses and driven to Black Bear State Park on the far side of Casler Lake for a school picnic."

Suddenly the thought hit me: why am I spilling my guts out about insignificant incidents that occurred to me over half a century ago? If it makes him happy, go with it, but first try to find out why he's so interested in Claire.

"What is this all about, Charlie? Please remind me about your interest in my youth, and moreover, this spooky interest in Claire Franklin."

"Dave, when we first met, you caught me going through a gray period of my life. There was no explanation for this behavior other than I had been overcome by a wave of depression and didn't realize it. The manner in which you extended friendship to me, and your small-town ways swung the tide. You asked earlier how I put a novel together and I kind of half explained. Maybe this will help you understand a little more of my thought process. Let me give you an example. When you were coaching, I imagine you installed new plays for your next opponent. I'm certain you knew what you wanted and could tell when the players ran it correctly. That same feeling follows me when I'm writing. Back then, I knew intuitively what I wanted and just wrote it down. After Betty died, that ability failed me.

"Since knowing you, I've sensed a return to form, but want to direct my energy to a new genre. I'm a city boy, always have been, while you're a small-town guy. Granted, you've been away from Casler most of your life, but that early experience has indelibly marked you forever. If you don't mind, I intend to use your early experiences as a springboard into a new venture. Slowly but surely the framework of a love story is germinating in this rusty old mind."

"I like hearing that, Charlie. Your effort will be totally different than anything you've done before. I'll look forward to reading it. I've got so many small town stories stored up; you can fill your novel with them. Where was I when I stopped talking?"

"You were telling about the school picnic at Casler Lake."

It took only moments for me to regroup. "Claire was different that day, but I couldn't place what it was. On the ride out to the park, she hardly talked to me, and unaccountably left me and walked off with some of her friends when we got there.

"Later, when we gathered to load the buses, she didn't speak for a moment, and then said, 'There's something I think you should know.' Her words slipped out, measured and slow. Fearing the worst and knowing what was at my doorstep, I can remember shuddering. Claire made a small 'get out of my life' gesture with her hand that told me in so many words she had dumped me. A glint of triumph in her eyes indicated she seemed pleased with herself. She turned on her heels and walked to another bus, never bothering to look back. It was obvious she had lost interest and wanted nothing more to do with me.

"I felt crushed and didn't know what to say. Charlie, looking back, I never suspected I'd feel so lousy. She had embarrassed me in front of my classmates and had put a new spin on an old game I wasn't familiar with. Ignorance is bliss if one doesn't know what your girlfriend has in mind, and what she had accomplished without saying a word I wasn't looking for. In a matter of seconds my simple life turned upside down, causing me to feel like I'd been run over by a truck. I can see it like it happened this morning. Believe me, I was speechless."

"I can't believe that mean bitch would do something like that!" Charlie pointed out.

His indignation caused me to laugh. "I wasn't smart enough to realize at the time what really happened. By the time we got back to school, I had reached my senses. It hit home, the love of my innocent young life had dumped me. The bad part of the ordeal was the silence. The kids knew what happened and appeared embarrassed.

"I was quiet at supper, causing my mother to ask what was troubling me. I didn't answer and merely went out to the backyard. Sitting down and lowering my head, I tried to sort out my confused emotions. Eventually, my father came out and sat down. He told me I should talk, so I did. I told him the whole story from how I liked her to what happened earlier in the day. Nothing was said for a minute or so until he spoke words I've never forgotten. He told me Claire was a nice girl from a good family, but losing her wasn't the end of good things in my future.

"When he mentioned Claire was a nice girl from a good family, I took exception to his words and told him how Claire had treated Catherine. To reinforce my feelings, I told him about my experience at Moving-up Day and flatly told him Claire was a mean person and I didn't want anything more to do with her.

"Dad pointed out that when you're young, nothing is forever and people change with time. He said I should think about making a bad situation work to my advantage. After he went back into the house, I continued trying to shape my thoughts and, at some point in that lonely backyard, arrived at an answer."

"What was your answer?"

"I decided at that moment to become a college football coach."

"Good choice. What motivated you to choose that line of work?"

"As a kid I listened to Dartmouth College football games on the radio. They were my team, and I lived and died with each of their games; still do as a matter-of-fact. Here's a tidbit for you."

I paused briefly to recall the facts.

"It was the game of the season and Dartmouth was playing Cornell at Ithaca. Dartmouth led throughout the game until Cornell punched over the winning touchdown on the last play of the game. I felt so bad I cried. After reviewing game films the next day, it was discovered that officials had inadvertently allowed Cornell a fifth down. Cornell graciously forfeited the game to Dartmouth. What happened is one of the great mysteries in college football history."

Charlie laughed. "You want me to believe that?"

"Absolutely, check it out."

"OK, I accept what you say as gospel. Tell you what, let's have another beer and you can tell me more about Claire."

"That sounds like an excellent thought, but why do you have this dogged interest in Claire?"

Charlie shrugged. "I have no idea, but there's something about her that appeals to me."

Chapter 7

"What do you think she looks like now?"

My thoughts caused me to break out laughing. "You're talking about Claire Franklin, aren't you?"

Charlie followed a shrug with a smile. "Who else but?"

"You must be deranged to ask such a question," I said amiably.

Charlie looked blankly out the window, apparently searching for an answer. He finally spoke up. "Lighten up, Dave; it's for my own selfish reasons."

Time passed with no words exchanged at our table until Charlie spoke. "Think of it as helping me write my next novel."

"Put that way, I'll try to come up with something on the fly. This is just a guess, mind you, but I'd say she retained her girlish good looks over the obvious surrender to old age we all suffer."

As my description spilled, he laughed. "I like that," and signaled me to continue.

"I imagine she's well-fed."

Charlie smiled. "You mean she's put on some weight."

"Not much, you understand, but enough to increase her dress size a number or two."

My friend was having a great time, the happiest I'd ever seen him. What the hell, I was enjoying creating this portrait, so why not embellish it for him? After all, Claire was Charlie's dream image, not mine.

"As far as wrinkles go, she didn't have many, probably some small folds around her mouth and eyes, but nothing significant. I'll bet she's showing hints of graying, but that only adds to the allure of her hair."

The smile on his face told me he relished the vivid picture I had stitched together of someone I'd not seen in over fifty years.

"Claire occasionally displayed a malicious side that marked anyone in her path. I remember an incident where she continually abused Catherine Hislop for no good reason. She became the object of Claire's fury. Catherine's family was desperately poor and everyone knew it. She had the identical look of the Okies that flooded Southern California during the depression. You know, something out of Steinbeck's *The Grapes of Wrath*."

Charlie nodded. "Yes, I remember the book."

"Here's an example of what small-town Maine was like when I was a kid. On the day I'm thinking about, fifth and sixth graders were scheduled for outdoor gym recess. It was open choice where we could use the playground equipment, or play organized games. There was a heavy rain that day, so we went to the gym.

"Mr. Gould, the gym teacher and coach came up with a beauty. He was going to teach us how to square dance. What a fiasco that turned out to be. Most of the girls could dance a little, but the boys, including me, thought dancing was sissy stuff and just screwed around. I guess the reason we did was because we didn't know how.

"Casler was such a small school, we knew everyone in grade school; there were only thirty in my grade. To understand what I'm describing, you have to picture what happened that day. Mr. Gould placed the girls in one row, the boys in another, with both lines facing each other. We had to cross over to the girl opposite us and she would be our partner. I lined up so Catherine was across from me. He placed four couples in a set, at which time we started learning how to square dance to a record by Two Tall Shields and His Casco Bay Boys. They were the most popular outfit in lower Maine. Charlie, isn't it amazing that I still recall that band?"

"That proves you haven't lost it to Alzheimer's. Now what about this square dancing?"

"Catherine was in the same predicament as the boys; she didn't know how to dance either. The boys grumbled like hell, but we got over it. I think the only casualty of that event was Catherine when Claire called out to her with a bite to her words, 'Hey, Hislop, you'll be able to dance if you wash your dirty feet'. Catherine brought her hands to her mouth and dashed out of the gym. I was too young to understand the hurt Claire's words carried with them. When we returned to our classroom, there sat Catherine with arms folded on her desk, her face buried, sobbing away."

Charlie's eyes flashed something I couldn't recognize. Finally, he spoke. "I'll use that material about square dancing and describe how country kids learned how to dance."

"Do you want to hear what I think?"

Charlie rubbed his chin. "Give it a rip."

"You got the hots for a ghost named Claire."

He looked at me without emotion. "That will be the day!"

His tight-lipped denial convinced me I had guessed correctly; he was taken with the apparition I had created. His fascination with Claire started with a tiny seed of yearning and gradually germinated into a full-blown curiosity.

Charlie appeared to shift his thoughts before speaking. "Believe me, I'm not haunted by some girl you grew up with, but I'm curious about what happened next."

"My friend, I've been out of touch with her since my high school days. How am I going to do that?"

"Take me back to the other side of time, and describe how you remember Claire. You told me a great deal about her, but there has to be more."

I thought of Claire with detachment, almost as if she had never existed. Soon however, long-forgotten thoughts came rushing to mind.

"Claire had a stylish charm that people liked but she occasionally displayed a flinty personality that permitted her snobbish side to show. Like a rose, here was a girl with many layers and a mind of her own. She was exceptionally bright and sailed through her courses with ease. The girl of your dreams was so preoccupied with her appearance she unconsciously preened all the time. You know, she was extremely vain." I smiled sarcastically. "Oh, vanity, has a name and she is called Claire Franklin. The overall Claire Franklin personality is easy to describe. She displayed a high-end beauty and, when in a crowd, people noticed her."

Charlie shook his head in dismay. "Dave, I went to high school with girls much like your Claire. They must have carried around a feeling of expectancy while harboring a secret dream that would someday lead them to a spirited kaleidoscope of fame and fortune."

"I like the way you talk, but sometimes I don't understand all that you say."

He shrugged happily. "Dave, it's what I do. I reserve my words to be placed on paper, but occasionally converse with a new acquaintance at the beach."

"Charlie, I've enjoyed talking about that image you have in your sights, but I have an appointment that needs attending to. I'll catch your act tomorrow. Instead of the bench, let's meet at BBC around noon and I'll treat you to lunch."

"I'll look forward to it, Dave. There's a hint of an idea for a novel bouncing around in my mind that won't go away. It centers on your Claire Franklin, my ghost if you will. I'd appreciate it if you could come up with a nugget about Casler and Claire all tied together. That would help me."

"I'll have something for you. Count on it."

Chapter 8

I revisited Casler in my mind and recalled memories of the junior prom incident I would reveal to Charlie. He was obviously waiting to hear my story while continually crossing and uncrossing his legs. To heighten his anticipation, I casually studied Martha's Vineyard in the distance. Finally, I started.

"Casler was a quiet community next to Casler Lake, about fifteen miles west of Portland. The high school is situated in the center of the village. As is the case in many small towns, the school was the center for numerous community activities, and I imagine it hasn't changed much. I mentioned earlier living in Casler and commuting to Portland my senior year to play sports. I still ran around with my Casler friends and somehow learned that Claire didn't have a date for the junior prom. You have to understand the Prom was the biggest school event of the year. The boys got dressed up, you know, shirt and tie, jacket or suit, the whole bloomin' bit. The girls, in turn, dolled up with evening gowns, high heels, fancy hairdos, the whole nine yards." I laughed at the thought of what happened so long ago. The memory came back like it happened yesterday.

"The guys even bought corsages for their dates. I can remember thinking it was odd that Claire didn't have a date, with her being up for prom queen, but that was her problem, not mine, so I, more or less, dropped the thought.

"One night she called the house and asked me if I'd be her date. Her request surprised me, but I readily agreed."

Charlie interrupted me with shining eyes. "I can see it coming, you and Claire got together again."

"It wasn't like that, believe me. We were good friends by then, and that arrangement worked well for both of us."

Charlie appeared disappointed. "I figured there was more to it than that."

"Hang around a little longer, there'll be more. The feeling you think of had long since passed. Getting back to the prom, I can remember dressing up the night of the dance in a new dark-blue pin-striped suit that made me look older than I was. I bought her an orchid for the dance. The reason I remember it is the damn flower cost me five bucks. My date had the only fancy corsage at the dance, while the rest of the girls were wearing two-dollar flowers." That declaration brought a smile to my face.

"When not playing a game, I bagged groceries at the Stop 'n' Shop in Portland on Saturdays. I know this is hard to believe, but my take-home pay for eight hours was a nickel under five dollars. I worked all day long to buy a flower that started to wilt in an hour, and came up five cents short of breaking even."

Charlie laughed after sipping his beer. "I can use that detail nicely, it's perfect. There's obviously more to the story."

"I don't have to tell you times were different then. Most of the faculty attended, as well as parents and some people from town. It was a big deal. The gym was decorated with streamers, balloons, and fancy artwork. Card tables were placed around the edge of the playing surface, leaving the center for dancing. A ten-piece band from Portland, the Blue Velvets, played popular dance music. You can understand the event was a special night in the lives of a bunch of small town kids."

"I never experienced anything like that back home. How did she look?" Charlie asked.

"Clair looked like a dream, wearing a beautiful royal blue evening gown with a fancy orchid. Her dress was cut a couple of inches above the ankle in front and dragged on the floor in back. Over her behind was a bustle or something that looked like a long narrow pillow. Apparently, it covered the seam that joined the bottom part of the dress to the top."

Pausing to sip my beer, Charlie anxiously encouraged me to continue.

"Crowning the queen was scheduled for eleven. Fifteen minutes before, the bandleader announced that queen candidates and their escorts should assemble in the hallway outside the gym. It's important that you form a picture of the scene in the hall. The five girls were standing together talking, while the guys were more or less in a group next to them. Mr. Starr, the junior advisor, came out and told us we'd have to line up. The girls started to move when the catastrophe hit. Time seemed to stand still."

Anticipation filled Charlie's eyes as a broad smile settled on his face.

"I didn't realize it at the time, but I had one foot resting on the train of Claire's dress. When she moved to line up, the back of her dress didn't move with her. After hearing the tearing sound, I realized the edge of doom was under my foot. You guessed it. The tuff pulled away and there stood my old girlfriend with her ass hanging out. Well, maybe not really out, but things weren't as they should have been. Her half-slip was pulled down so you could see the top of her girdle. Clare looked hard at me with shock in her eyes but didn't speak; she was that shocked. I sensed the incident was a problem, maybe even a big deal. It was obvious she was angry as hell and who could blame her? At that moment, time really stood still."

Charlie was all smiles when he asked, "Did her nose wrinkle?"

"You better believe it," I happily replied.

My writer friend laughed so hard, the patrons at the bar turned to look at him. He was in such uncontrolled laughter; they followed suit, enjoying whatever the moment was before they finally returned to their drinks.

It took a few moments before he got himself under control, wiping away tears before asking, "What happened next?"

"It was a moment that one hopes never happens, but sometimes does. I felt like walking away from the mess I had created but realized I had to stay and face the music. I remember struggling helplessly, searching for something to say and drawing a blank. I had become the boy in the black hat."

Charlie appeared totally absorbed in my narrative. "And then?"

"My friends understood it was a bad situation, but still laughed until their girlfriends set them straight. Mr. Starr immediately left us in search of help, leaving an uneasy silence settling around the hallway. All the girls, except Brenda Emery, stood glaring at me without saying a word. Brenda marched up to me with steam coming out of her ears. She literally screamed, 'Dave

Foster, you're such a horse's ass! I can't believe you.' I closed my eyes and tried to remember when I was happy, but failed.

"The thing that turned the disaster into an, oh, happy night was the fact Brenda was the Methodist minister's daughter. A gentle, kind person, her anger shocked me to the point I started laughing. Soon the guys followed accordingly, and then the girls joined in. Even though Brenda's anger continued to grow, she eventually laughed with the others. Although Claire was the victim with her ass peeking out of her torn dress, she laughed, not like the others, but she was a good sport about it."

Charlie had now dissolved into another fit of uncontrolled laughter and once again drew the attention of those at the bar. A friend from down the street called out, "Dave, I don't know what you're telling this bird, but it must be something special."

"It is, buddy. It's nothing like you've ever heard in your life," Charlie said through peels of laughter. Once his wild ride through jocularity concluded, he signaled me to continue.

"Charlie, I'm sorry to disappoint you, but fortunately, Miss Riddle the homemaking teacher was at the dance and took Claire up to her room for some temporary repairs. Thirty minutes later, the dress was repaired and Claire was crowned prom queen, though she stood a little funny while receiving her crown. That's a fact, all of it. Now that I've provided you with some comic relief for the day, I have to hit the road."

"Is that how it ended?"

"Well, there's more. I'll tell you about it another time," I said while preparing to leave.

"Let's have another beer and you can finish this great story," he said in a pleading voice.

"No, two beers is enough for the day. Besides, Stop 'n' Shop is calling."

I walked away leaving a disappointed Charlie studying a fresh glass of beer.

Chapter 9

"Good morning, Dave. It feels like another scorcher on the way," Charlie said while settling next to me. After discussing baseball scores from the previous night, he changed the subject.

"There's something I want to run by you. Having read my nautical and mystery stories, you're familiar with my style. Since we've become friends, my desire to write has been resurrected, and I'm considering writing a love story. Do you have any thoughts?"

"Judging by your questions about my youth, I guessed you'd pick up the pen and start your career again. That's great to hear, but what do you know about writing a love story?"

A long pause passed before he replied. "Dave, I was married forty-five years, and I learned a great deal about the subject from Betty."

"Charlie, please believe me that inconsiderate comment wasn't meant to hurt you. I'm sorry for saying it."

"That's all right, things happen. Getting back to my writing, I intend to write a novel that will incorporate other people's experiences with romance. I've stored much of what you've talked about from your earlier days, and I expect to enlarge on my file before I begin. Of course, Betty will be brought into the picture, but I don't know how far I'll go with her image. Claire Franklin will play an important role, but I don't know when and where I'll fit her into the lot. Does that make sense?"

"To me it does, but don't take my word for it. How do you plan to approach it?"

"I honestly don't know. I'll probably muddle through until something clicks. There is one thing that keeps coming up in my thoughts. Do you know what happened to that little girl in grade school you talked about earlier? You know, the poor one."

I fell silent while organizing my memory.

"As a matter-of-fact, I do. This would be Catherine Hislop you're talking about."

"Would you tell me about her?"

"There's nothing I'd rather do. I was downtown in Portland just before heading for graduate school in North Carolina when the urge hit me to have a hot dog and root beer for lunch. I went into Woolworth's because they served frosty Hires root beer that came from a barrel-shaped cooler. Do you remember those old brown tankers?" Charlie nodded he did.

"After some small talk with the waitress, much to my surprise, she asked me if I recognized her. A hint of someone from my past pierced my mind, but I drew a blank with the flashback. I had to admit I didn't.

"She smiled and told me she was Dorothy Hislop, Catherine's sister.

"I tried not to, but sensed my voice inflection changed to a curious tone. 'So you work here?' Kind of a stupid question, I thought, but it was the best I could come up with at the time.

"I can remember Dorothy nodded yes and mentioned how she worked days and attended night school at the University of Maine Extension in town. Her goal was to become an English teacher. I told her that was terrific and she'd be a good one.

"She mentioned that it hadn't been easy, but a strong determination carried her through the tough times. Dorothy brought up how most people remember the good times in their history, but that was not the case with her. She asked me if I could understand her feelings.

"Obviously I could, and remember telling her that the pain she suffered was far different from anything I ever experienced. Charlie, I was too curious to let it go without telling her how I somehow felt connected to her and Catherine, and would like to hear her story.

"I'll never forget her answer. 'For you I will,' and then she asked, 'have you ever been really hungry?'

"I nodded no, but wondered where she was headed.

"She replied immediately, 'We were always starved, and that's the truth. My mother fried bread in grease and sent us off to school with that as our lunch.'

"I asked her how her family could eat unheated bread loaded with grease?

"She answered, 'eating something is better than eating nothing at all. One day I caught my little brother Jimmy eating dirt. Can you imagine growing up with a diet like that? That's the reason Catherine had boils on her legs; not from eating dirt you see, but from the lack of proper nourishment.'

"The mention of boils brought back thoughts of a little girl sitting next to me with mean-looking sores on her legs.

"Dorothy's voice snapped me out of my meandering into the past. 'Dave, I have to get back to work. Stop back and we can continue our talk. My lunch break starts at one. It's been nice seeing you.'

"Two days later I again found myself in a booth at Woolworth's resuming my conversation with Dorothy. Our talk finally came around to her brief days in Casler.

"'All the Hislop kids heard the constant ridicule that came our way, but the younger ones didn't really understand it. We were treated like one would treat a skunk at a lawn party. Oh, the bad talk hurt, not that it mattered because I was too tough for it to get me down.' Dorothy paused to sip her coffee.

"I asked her, how Catherine was getting along.

"She told me, 'Catherine was doing great, but back then she was different than the others in the family. Even as a young kid living in a world of delusions, she was a little lady with her gentle ways. Our family's plight, coupled with the constant teasing she encountered at school, practically destroyed her. I believe there are certain times in a person's life when anguish overcomes them and they are helpless to move on. She was like a fragile tree in a wind storm, going through life alone—until you came along.' Dorothy looked at me with tear-filled eyes. 'She got better because you made it so.'

"I told her that wasn't the case, that we were friends and nothing more.

"She strongly replied, 'That may be so, but you were the only person outside our family who was her friend.'

"I merely shrugged, not knowing what to say. Dorothy picked up the tempo of her narrative by talking about the Hislop clan.

"'My family had two choices. One was to throw in the towel, the second, continue struggling. Thankfully, my parents chose the latter, and we helped each other as best we could along the way. Dad was a mechanic at a textile factory when he became a casualty of the times, the Depression, you know. For the next ten years the kids kept coming, but he couldn't find a job to support us. As a result we continued to get poorer. Wherever we lived, the sweet bird of plenty never flew over our house.'

"Dorothy left the booth to get refills of coffee and soon returned, smiling.

"'People were so preoccupied with their own problems, they didn't seem to have time for those who had fallen into the cracks of social decline. Many families needed a second chance, and the Hislops topped the list. The elusive reprieve finally came when Dad somehow heard about a paper mill job in a small town some eighty miles north of here. He hitchhiked to Farmington to interview for the job and miraculously was hired. You probably know the town I'm talking about.'

"A slight nod of my head indicated I did."

"'The boss that hired my father was a good man. He gave Dad enough money to take the bus back to Casler, buy work shoes, clothing and move the family up north. Suddenly, the Hislops gradually came out of our funk, and realized what many people considered a normal life. Incredibly, we had risen from the ashes of abject poverty.'

"I sat captivated by the story of a family's escape from desperation told by a survivor. There were questions that needed answering, so why not ask them, I thought.

"Charlie, I kept hearing remarkable stories about the Hislop family, and then asked about Catherine. I also asked about her side of the story.

"'I'm well on my way about getting ahead of this rat race, but forget about me. She's the shining star of the Hislop family. After graduating from high school, with high honors I might add, she entered Farmington State as a library science major. I helped her when I could, which wasn't much, but after all she was my sister. I'm so proud of her I can hardly stand it,' she said while blinking away tears.

"Dorothy stood up. 'David, I have to go back to work. Stop in and see me before you head for North Carolina.'

"After she returned to work, I drove out to Casler to spend a couple of days with my parents. Three days later I drove the fifteen miles into Portland, thinking back to when I made the daily trip to play football for Portland Central. Thinking about football reminded me that pre-season practice was starting within the week and I should stop to see Dorothy before leaving for UNC.

"I raised my hand to greet her while settling on the only empty seat at the lunch counter. My gaze shifted to a young woman seated next to me, but quickly returned to watch Dorothy efficiently serve a customer.

"She displayed an exceptional smile while serving me coffee. 'David, do you recognize this young lady?'

"I turned to study the woman just mentioned. Her simple good looks took my breath away. My thoughts raced back to grade school. I had never seen the gorgeous smile she offered before, but the image of a somber little sixth-grader came to mind. I was so stunned it took moments to speak.

"It truly is you, Catherine," I haltingly stammered.

"She replied with a lovely smile. 'Hello, David. You were my sixth grade knight in shining armor.' Her eyes sparkled in a teasing way.

"Catherine was sensational, without a doubt a knockout. I could hardly catch my breath while studying her beauty. She was a true connection to an oft forgotten memory of my life thirteen years earlier.

"We adjourned to an empty booth where she proceeded to inquire about my days after Casler. I explained my three years at Potham, four years in the Air Force during the Korean War, and my final year in college after returning from the service. When I told her about heading for the University of North Carolina as a graduate assistant, she seemed happy for me. I can remember her telling me I'd be good at coaching. As we talked, the thought came over me that Catherine was the prototype of a gracious lady.

"The conversation shifted to her experiences since Casler. She spoke of her days in Farmington and at the college in town. Dreams of finding a place in her heart quickly evaporated when

Catherine informed me she had married an assistant professor at Farmington State. After hearing of her marital status, I felt crushed. I actually got mad as hell that some bastard had married this lovely woman. After that childish thought passed, I rationalized that it was better to know than not know.

"We parted company with Catherine telling me it was a treat seeing me again. She asked too, for me to keep a good thought of Dorothy and her. She returned to her home in Upstate Maine while I headed for Chapel Hill in North Carolina. So, there you are, end of story."

"I can do something with that. There are some questions I'd like to ask," Charlie said assuredly.

"Fire away."

"You rendered a general portrait of Catherine, but I can't physically picture her. Can you help me with that?"

"At that time, she was of medium height, with a slight build. She had nice teeth with a smooth complexion to match, and her hair was blonde. There it is in a nice package, Catherine Hislop or whatever her name was when I last saw her. Are you in love with her, too?" I smiled broadly.

Charlie laughed too. "Not really, I just needed to put her in my memory bank. There's something else I don't understand. You mentioned being surprised that Catherine was married. Didn't you notice her wedding band?"

His question stumped me for a moment. "Guess I was so taken with looking at her, I didn't check her hand," I said lamely.

"Good answer. I have to leave. A college buddy teaches at Bridgewater State; it's just up the road from here. Have you heard of it?"

"Know it well. We played them in football when I was coaching."

"Anyway, he has tickets for the Red Sox vs. Bridgeton Gulls three-game series. Fred and his wife are treating me to a nice weekend."

"Have a good time," I said as he walked away.

Chapter 10

The sun was thirty minutes from sunrise when I settled on the porch with a cup of coffee and Charlie's novel. Comfortably seated, the story my friend had written carried me away to a world of which I knew nothing.

The sun god rose red and hot, ready to turn his supreme heat on the Heights.

At the time I didn't realize this day would be different than any I'd ever known. Charlie's tale of intrigue was thoroughly enjoyable and intense, only to be interrupted by a figure on the sidewalk.

When I looked up, something about the woman heading my way reminded me of what I thought Claire Franklin would look like in her late sixties. Of all the thoughts that crossed my mind during an average day, the thought of an old high school girlfriend walking toward me at Falmouth Heights Beach seemed totally absurd.

Moments later, I recognized the walk—it *was* Claire. This well-groomed woman, elegant and stately in casual beach attire, was effortlessly moving my way with a silky gait, a model of grace. I couldn't take my eyes off this poetry in motion. The memory of Claire and Casler suddenly consumed my thoughts. A massive rush of excitement grabbed at the fond memory of a girl with an overpowering personality from my Casler days. I noticed the same dark brown hair I remember from earlier days, only now touched ever so lightly with a wisp of silver. Her hair was pulled back and secured by a barrette to keep it in place, reminiscent of her days as a high school cheerleader. It was obvious Claire possessed a beauty that defied her age, quickening hearts as easily at sixty-nine as she did when she was seventeen.

It was fifty-two years ago, a lifetime, since I last saw her. Nothing is ever the same, I cautioned myself, but one ever knows what will happen with such an extraordinary encounter. Who knows? This may be the day my life turns around.

Taking a deep breath, my words came out in a rush. "Hey there, stranger, can I buy you a cup of coffee?"

Claire directed her penetrating gaze toward the porch. It was evident she was still proud and strong-willed, her brown eyes told me that. We looked at each other without speaking, a surprised look settling on her face. It was the first time since Casler we'd made eye contact. If I thought of her over the years, it was with detachment, almost as if she hadn't existed; suddenly here she stood. The intervening years had been good to her.

I took a deep breath and tried one more time. "Hello."

An awkward moment passed before she spoke, delight registering on her face. "Dave Foster, I can't believe my eyes!" She spoke with a gentle dignity. "Small world, isn't it?"

A sweet voice from the past accompanied by a brilliant smile crossing her face was one I'd not seen for over half a century. She hurriedly moved to the porch with outstretched arms. I could feel her body tense while holding me in a hug, after which she planted a feathery kiss on my cheek.

Directing her to a chair, my words flowed with ease. "Claire, history finds a way of repeating itself."

For a good half-hour, a quiet conversation ensued with common memories derived from our shared upbringing in a small town. I had a feeling this encounter was more than a chance meeting.

"Claire, I'm embarrassed to ask, but here goes. You mentioned that you live in Virginia, but here you are on Cape Cod in Falmouth. Are you on vacation?"

She gave me her million dollar smile. "Not quite, but almost."

My puzzled look caused her brilliant smile to radiate across the porch. "I'm here helping my thirty-five year old baby. Bobby just bought a home on Worchester Court." She waved to the street that runs into Grand Avenue. "He's my youngest and I watch over him like a mother hen. All my kids are bright, but he's the sharpest. Bobby did his undergraduate and graduate work in marine biology at the University of Miami, ultimately receiving his PhD. He moved around until he accepted the position of associate director at the Woods Hole Oceanographic Institution.

"Very simply, I'm here helping to put his house in order. He has five children, just like his mother and needless to say, his wife has all she can handle." Claire laughed while holding her hands up. "It's easy to see I've been working by the look of these ugly things."

It became evident that maturity had softened her forceful personality. The moment I sought finally presented itself. I asked about her post-high school days.

She shrugged helplessly while biting her lips in a nervous gesture. "My life got away from me."

I didn't understand her meaning, but I waited patiently for her to elaborate.

"After graduating from high school, I attended the University of Virginia."

Her choice of college piqued my interest. "That's a long distance from home. How in the world did you ever settle on Virginia?"

She appeared to retreat inside herself for moments on end before answering.

"My family went on vacation to Virginia the summer before my senior year. During the trip we visited Monticello and the University of Virginia in Charlottesville. I was quite taken with the college and decided to attend; it was that simple. I majored in pre-med and had every intention of attending medical School. That all changed when I met Mr. Right at a fraternity party my junior year. Joe Cummins was a dream and, just like in the movies, he swept me off my feet. A brute of a man, he played football and lacrosse and was considered a big man on campus."

Her eyes, filled with tears, misted as she drifted into the past, reflecting for a moment before continuing in a hushed voice.

"Joe was handsome beyond belief and never looked back at anything. Extroverted to a fault, he garnered high honors in everything he touched, effortlessly gliding through his studies at Virginia. After graduation, we married and moved to a small city west of Washington, D.C. Leesburg is a charming colonial city that retains much of its early charm. Perhaps you know it."

I nodded yes.

"That was my second mistake," she said with a grimace.

Claire left out what her first mistake was, but I couldn't help guessing. Maybe it was the thought she hadn't become a doctor or maybe there was something about her marriage that troubled her. It was none of my business and I left it at that.

"Joe was recruited by the CIA while in college and no sooner had we settled in Leesburg than he was sent to the farm or, to be more precise, Camp Perry. After he completed training, the merry-go-round started for me," she recalled uncomfortably. "It seemed he was away from home much of the time. I got pregnant soon after arriving in Leesburg. It seems from that moment on I remained as they say, barefoot and pregnant." She rolled her eyes, after which an embarrassing quiet settled on the porch.

It seemed a bit unnatural that Claire would reveal such intimate details of her life to me so quickly; me, almost a complete stranger now. I searched her face for a clue as to how we might proceed.

Further words weren't needed for me to understand she'd been searching for that special person she could trust who would provide her comfort and a friendly ear. Her candor indicated I was the one who fit the bill.

Claire spoke with a half-embarrassed smile. "In ten years, I produced five babies who proved to be exceptional athletes and stellar students. That's one thing I was good at, raising children. What do you think of that?"

"I'd say it's quite an achievement. You still look attractive as you were in high school."

Claire laughed. "Dave Foster, you still carry on like you used to," she said smoothly.

Her comment made me smile. "Yeah, I guess I have a little of that left in me. But I'm curious, what happened next?"

Believing her words would fail, Claire rubbed her neck until she picked up her story with a sigh. "In the real world, things don't always happen the way you planned. Over the years, Joe worked with numerous women whom I believe were more than just friends. I later discovered he was a confirmed womanizer and totally amoral, a cold detached man. Though, to his credit, he went through the motions of being a dedicated father and husband to the outside world."

She divulged a part of her history that moved me to ask a delicate question. "I was about to ask, if that was the case, why ..."

Claire raised her hand to interrupt, her lips forming a straight line. "Why didn't I leave him? I skated around the truth, protecting myself before I finally faced the facts." Her shoulders settled into a hopeless shrug. "Looking back, I was old-fashioned and wanted to make the marriage work. But I felt trapped."

A pained look settled on her face followed by a catch in her throat.

"There were no options to speak of at the time. Have you ever heard the expression, 'take an hour and you'll get over it'? Well, it didn't work that way. It wasn't possible. Claire Cummins just wasn't strong enough to leave him and go out on her own." She thrust her hands in front of her, palms up. "I had the kids to think about, and that thought caused my life to become an unspoken lie to protect them. It was one of my darkest periods. I knew people talked but as the years went by, I became indifferent to what they said."

I felt the need to break the rhythm of her unhappy story. Searching for something to say that would momentarily distract her, I finally suggested a repast.

"Claire, the morning is heating up, so excuse me for a moment while I bring us something cold to drink." Several minutes later, I returned with two frosty glasses of iced tea. A few quiet moments passed between us until Claire spoke up.

"That was a chaotic time in my life. One I can only describe in one word: hopeless." Her eyes reflected a still-present sadness.

"Claire, mistakes and misfortune come with living life."

A sudden torrent of tears followed. I felt her pain and didn't like the fact that I had encouraged her to speak of her mosaic of misery.

"I'm saddened to hear of your misfortune."

"Dave, forget those thoughts. The story of the next chapter of my life is rosier. For the first time in years, I'm able to converse with someone with an established link back to Casler, a time when my life was stable and happy. Now, for the sunny side of my life," she laughed heartily.

Claire still had that same stunning laugh she had as a kid, I reminded myself with a smile.

"I was never pressed for money when I was married. In fact, there was more than I ever needed. After Bobby was born, Joe built a five-bedroom house in town that was the jewel of a charming neighborhood. I lived in a lovely house that wasn't a home and all the time realized I wasn't in control of myself. At that point of my life, the thought of living through another day was daunting."

She stopped talking, seemingly to rearrange her thinking while I sat in silence digesting her story.

Claire's tale of difficulty tossed my emotions around in a way that troubled me. It seemed the shoe was on the other foot. She had suffered through the antics of an unfaithful husband who reflected her style from an earlier age of loving them and leaving them. The thought that it serves her right interrupted my thinking. Another thought immediately surfaced, contrary to the first. In my rush to judgment, I had forgotten that she was my friend in Casler. Who was I not to be a friend now?

"My situation suddenly took a turn from hopeless to encouraging. Joe inexplicably bought an enchanting cottage unbeknownst to me. It's located in a quiet beach community called Sands Beach, nestled next to Chesapeake Bay. I was furious with him over his underhanded method of not discussing the purchase with me but later his reasoning surfaced—much later, in fact."

Claire's brown eyes indicated anguished thoughts. "Our life together was like two passing ships in the night. Joe was going his way, me being nothing more than the caretaker of his kids and home. Over the next few years, we, meaning the kids and I, spent more and more time at the Sands Beach house. Then one day Joe came to the beach house to talk, or at least that's what the bastard called it."

I never heard her say one single swear word, however her use of bastard caused me to chuckle to myself. She blankly looked at me laughing, and then followed my lead without missing a beat.

"You've heard the expression, 'the problem with bad news is, more usually follows'. Well, that wasn't true in my case. Joe announced he was reinventing himself with the help of a woman he truly loved. When he asked for a divorce, I quickly granted his wish and in the next moment showed him the door. After he left, I felt simultaneously hurt and relieved."

Chapter 11

Claire grew silent, seemingly lost in thought, her eyes shining with tears. "Joe killed something in me when he left. After his departure, I felt myself living day-to-day in slow motion. I'm resilient, always have been, and, at that time, decided to set my mind in order and forge ahead. As I think back, my social life needed some attention, but I had no idea how to improve things." She smiled with a distant look in her eyes.

We sat in silence, the depth of her bad luck leaving me unsettled.

Suddenly, her face sparkled with delight. "It was unfair that I found myself in this untenable situation and I decided to make the best of a bad predicament. There were too many ugly memories associated with the Leesburg house for me to stay there. I needed to look for something but, I didn't know what. Trying to reinvent myself would be wistful thinking if I didn't act immediately. Dave, depressing times call for desperate measures. The next thing I knew, the house was up for sale. It was a big decision for me but helped me rise from the ashes of a bad marriage."

Her story sounded like something Charlie would write. I felt her rush of excitement and couldn't wait to hear more.

"What happened then, Claire?"

"Would you believe it? The house sold in three days. There was a seller's market at the time with houses going for premium prices. As part of the divorce settlement, Joe gave me the Leesburg house and the Sands Beach cottage plus half of our savings."

"Wow," I said. "You did well by that agreement. It appears your ex gave away the shop."

My reaction caused Claire to display a broad smile. "Indeed, but don't feel too badly for him. The woman he married has more money than brains. There he sits enjoying the good life in a fashionable house overlooking the harbor of Annapolis, living off her money, the dirty leach!" She laughed through another broad smile.

Carried away by her history with Joe, I asked about her new life.

"I shipped items that were special to me to Sands Beach. You understand, bits and pieces of furniture, some of the kids' possessions, and my personal treasures. Everything else in the house went to a household jobber who carted it away. I took one last look at the Leesburg house and never looked back." She gave me an enormous smile.

She still has iron in her blood, I thought.

"I'd like to hear about where you live."

"Where I live is not a pretentious beach house, far from it. It's an old-fashioned cottage. Dave, the houses along the beach comprise a neighborhood much like the ones we knew in Casler. The Sands Beach community is situated beside a mile-long crescent of sun-bleached white sand that runs between the water and a narrow country road. My house is on the other side, along with probably fifty others."

"How long did it take you to settle in?"

"The change of scenery and new setting was a challenge I had to face but the sheltered life I lived didn't help. I didn't handle the change very well in the beginning but after several weeks a soothing peace settled over me that I'd not experienced in years. I remember thinking this move had better work because it was the only thing I had going for me."

"What are your summers like down there?"

"When I moved to Sands Beach, summer was at its peak. "I'll tell you no lie, they're hot, but the prevailing breeze tempers the intense heat to a pleasant atmosphere."

"What's your favorite time of day?"

"I have two, early morning and after the sun sets. I wake up before the rooster crows. As you know, old habits always seem to stay around."

I nodded in agreement.

"Hearing the sounds drifting up from the beach makes waking up worthwhile. I love listening to the water washing against the beach and smelling fresh air drifting through the house. It's wonderful. The mornings are so serene, it's startling; almost like a window to my Casler past. On many occasions a light mist under a heavy overcast sky settles over the area. Even though the setting has a dreary feel to it, the sun quickly burns it off and leaves a distinct impression of a bright day on its way. I'm captivated by the simple beauty that greets me on most mornings."

"It sounds like you're describing an appealing beach scene, and it's all in your front yard. In fact, I can picture it."

Claire nodded. "Yes, to me, it's an Alice-in-Wonderland setting. As the sun sets, I take to my front porch. The dark waters begin to churn, generating a hint of salt that fills the air. The sound of squawking seagulls and the occasional car passing by are about the only intrusions interrupting the quiet. There are walkers of all sizes and descriptions that pass by, many of them couples from the neighborhood. That's when the loneliness settles in," she said with a sigh.

"You must have a circle of friends to fill this void."

"I do, Dave, but there's something lacking in my life."

"You mean a man?"

"That's exactly what I mean. There's a man down the street whom I'm close to. Jack O'Brennan is a retired detective of the city police force in Bridgeton who runs a one-man detective agency. Jack gained a degree of notoriety by solving two cold cases where killings dated back many years. The Bridgeton newspaper described him as "The Tracer of Unsolved Murders" after the old radio program, *Mr. Keene, Tracer of Lost Persons.*"

The name Jack O'Brennan triggered my thoughts to race back to what Charlie Jamison told me about the source of some of his novels. Could it be possible that both Claire and Charlie are talking about the same person? I told myself it was impossible and to forget it.

"As a matter of fact, I substituted him as the man in my life. His wife Jeanette, is my closest friend and leads an interesting and enviable life. She runs the most popular restaurant on the west side of Chesapeake Bay, The Red Squire. It's a lovely eatery twenty miles east of Bridgeton. The Squire provides shore dining at modest prices that most families can afford. He and Jeanette helped me sort out my life when I first moved to the beach. Jack has a gift for knowing things about people and offers advice that's simple and works."

The thought finally settled in that Claire was playing nice with this O'Brennan. I looked intensely at her with my eyes revealing my understanding of the true nature of her relationship with her best friend's husband.

She read my look and then fervently declared, "No, it isn't like that nor will it ever be!" Her firmly-set jaw prompted me to laugh.

The conversation started to wane when I suggested we walk to the corner for lunch. A slight nod provided her answer.

Chapter 12

We talked of the breathtaking beauty of Cape Cod while casually walking to the restaurant. After ordering, Claire directed the conversation in my direction.

She smiled while tilting her head. "Dave, all I've done is talk about what's happened to me; now it's your turn. Tell me about your life since leaving Casler."

As my history unfolded, I sensed Claire becoming increasingly absorbed in my narrative. I talked of Jane, starting with our first meeting in Chapel Hill to her death three years ago.

Claire took in a deep breath, and then heavily exhaled. Several minutes passed before she spoke.

"I'm immensely saddened by your loss, and 'I'm sorry' is all I can say."

Pushing ahead, I mentioned my three children and their lives after leaving the nest. The next ten minutes covered my coaching career at Potham. We sat in silence while the waitress served our lunch, Claire's eyes narrowing in my direction with a critical stare.

"You could've done so much with your life, but instead spent your entire working career as a football coach."

The Claire I grew up with wasn't vindictive, sharp-tongued maybe, but never heartless. Was this another side of her I'd only observed at the expense of others? It might have been her tone more than the criticism that prompted me to flinch. I could feel the color rising on my face. The hard-edged glance I directed at her made clear how badly I felt. Her comment surprised me.

Realizing the damage she had done with her barbed comment, she raised a hand to her mouth.

A voice in my head told me to control my emotions and think rather than speak my mind. I realized my anger would surface later, but sensed the matter should be forgotten. I gracefully accepted her rebuke.

I momentarily looked back to earlier days at Casler High. There were certain incidents in my past that never changed and Claire being Claire was one of them. While looking at her, images of Jane flashed in my mind. I wondered how she would have handled this awkward situation.

Regardless of what my thoughts advised, my heart reacted differently, compelling me to answer.

"You want me to feel better after such a comment. In truth, the thought never crossed my mind to pursue anything other than coaching."

A half-embarrassed expression crossed her face while releasing a long sigh.

Giving her no chance to reply, I forged ahead. "I wanted to be a football coach from the time I was a kid and listened to Dartmouth College games. If you recall, I transferred to Portland Central to learn the game. What we have here is a difference of opinion regarding my life endeavor.

"By the way, there's something else you overlooked. Think back for a moment to when we were in school. When Friday nights rolled around in the fall, your dad drove into Portland to see me play. Amazingly, Dr. Van Fleet took time off from his busy schedule to go in with him. Your mother kept the store open while they were gone."

My recollection caused Claire to smile.

"There's something else," I offered. "Did you know your father continually encouraged me to take up a career in coaching? Unlike you, he would have applauded my coaching efforts."

Claire sat staring into space, blinking away tears that had filled her eyes. Directing a pleading glance at me, she helplessly raised her hands, and then quickly returned them to her lap. Swallowing with difficulty, she spoke in a whisper.

"David Foster, please forgive me for those nasty words. I know they hurt, and for that I'm sorry." She lowered her head in a contrite manner, releasing a cascade of tears that marked her light brown blouse with dark spots.

"Let it go, Claire; it's water over the dam and best forgotten."

She had won the battle but I had won the war. My insignificant victory was of little comfort to me when looking at a weeping Claire. I signaled our server for the check.

Glancing at our untouched lunch, the waitress asked, "Wasn't the food satisfactory?" I replied that everything was fine with the service; it was just that my friend wasn't feeling well, and had lost her appetite.

We walked back in silence. Approaching the beach house, a thought intruded into my muddled brain: Claire was desperately lonely while pushing through life without a go-to friend. Well, from now on, I'm going to be that special person, I told myself. She obviously feels embarrassed, and wants to hide after what she thought was a devastating moment.

"Dave, it'd been a pleasant surprise meeting you after so many years, but I feel so irritated and, yes, disappointed in myself for causing you such obvious pain over the unthinkable comment I made at lunch. Please forgive me. It's appropriate for me to walk away before doing any further damage."

Her eyes filled with tears while turning to walk down the sidewalk.

"Claire, you listen to me before walking away! We're never going to look back at what was from this instant on, I won't hear of it! This may not be easy to hear, but there are certain circumstances in life that don't change. You know exactly what I'm talking about, and if you don't, let me spell them out for you. Our days in Casler were spent generating a built-in antagonism by occasionally belittling each other with demeaning words. I'm going to change that right now. Don't draw any conclusions about romance, because that thought never entered my mind."

I'm too old and have too many memories of Jane to enter into a relationship with the likes of Claire. I can't explain why she intimidates me, but she always did and still does. Treat her as a close friend, and leave it at that for your own benefit, I counseled myself.

Without taking a step, she stared at me in disbelief.

"Now that you've heard what's on my mind, I'm not anticipating any further damage. It will not be prudent for you to walk away now; not my words but yours. We need time to cool down and become real friends, so let's start now.

We can't do all that today, so tell me where your son lives and I'll be at his front door at eight-thirty in the morning to take you out to breakfast. That will give us the time we need to regroup. Does that make sense?"

She nodded yes in a confused state.

"We didn't eat lunch this afternoon for obvious reasons; however, we're going to catch up right now. I'm going to make you a luscious lobster salad in a New England bun sliced on the top. I'll bet you haven't had one since leaving Casler."

"You're right. Now that you mention it, I have thoughts of our gang streaming into Richardson's drug store on Fridays for his lobster rolls. Dave, growing up where we were raised was a delight, and talking to you brings back memories of an important compartment of my life."

Thirty minutes later Claire wiped her mouth delicately with a napkin. "That was wonderful. We have nothing like that back home in Virginia. I'm going to persuade Jeanette to add it to her menu."

Claire made it clear she had to get back to Bobby's house, allowing our conversation of our high school days to linger and be savored until another time.

Chapter 13

My eyes zeroed in on Charlie walking briskly toward the bench. Seeing it was empty, he stopped to look around. For my own selfish reasons, I wanted him to turn around and leave, but that wasn't meant to be. A spur-of-the moment impulse caused me to call out to him, "Charlie, over here."

As he walked toward the porch, the thought surfaced that, in the grand scheme of events, there wasn't a better time for Charlie to meet someone as different and engaging as Claire; she was all that and more.

I asked him about his baseball trip to Boston, and then motioned him to a seat.

He shrugged. "The Red Sox beat the Gulls in all three games."

At that moment, Claire got his attention. In return, she directed an unyielding glance at him with hooded eyes and a crinkled nose.

The thought crossed my mind: "I wonder if he's thinking what I am?"

Charlie smiled while settling into a Kennedy rocker, giving Claire a long appraising look. His eyes told me he was smitten by her appearance. Running a hand through his brush cut he blew his breath out in delight. "Love what I see, Dave. I haven't met this beauty before, have I?"

"Claire Cummins, meet Charlie Jamison."

"It's great to meet you." He couldn't hide his elation, nor did he try. "Dave, is this the Claire Franklin from Casler you told me about?"

"One and the same," I replied with the slight show of a grin.

Claire appeared marginally interested while smiling at Charlie. "Thank you for staring," she said flirtatiously. "You are more than generous." Claire Franklin Cummins appeared pleased with her response.

Obsessed with an image devised from my memory, he was now seeing his mental creation in living color.

Her comment caused a mischievous smile to settle on his face. "Dave, put purely and simply, your guest is absolutely gorgeous."

What I'm seeing is pretty racy stuff for two people who just recently met. There's no accounting for Charlie's reaction to Claire. Last week, I met a man seemingly devastated over the loss of his soul mate, now the same man is behaving like a teenager, judging by the foolish way he's acting. Maybe there's an unwritten protocol about finding a companion when one reaches my age. It was obvious he was positioning himself to put a new spin on the same old game of boy meets girl, I mentally observed.

My observation caused me to laugh, drawing curious glances from my guests.

"Friends, the sun is heating the porch up, so excuse me while I get something cool to drink."

During the time I mixed drinks, their quiet conversation, sprinkled with nervous laughter, drifted into the kitchen. It seemed Claire listened while Charlie, the story teller, carried on.

Several minutes later I returned with three frosty glasses of iced tea, placing them on a serving table between my visitors. Claire reached for a glass with a knockout smile directed at Charlie, presenting him with a clear view of a sensational cleavage. He raised an eyebrow while lifting his glass to me in salute. Was her gesture inadvertent or a deliberate display of seduction? I wondered. Whatever it was, the magic moment certainly captured Charlie's attention.

My career in football taught me how to adjust to surprises, but seeing them hit it off in thirty short minutes was a new experience.

At that moment a strange thought crossed my mind. Why was I so consumed with Claire in high school? The answer came as quickly as the question. My attraction to her was nothing more than a classic case of puppy love. It was nothing like I had experienced with Jane. There obviously is a wide gulf between adolescent love and the real thing.

I felt swept up as I listened to their chatter. It seemed Charlie was about to start life anew. Observing his resurrection was something to behold, prompting me to suspect they were heading for a romance on the fly. It was as evident as the lettering on a movie theater marquee.

"Gentlemen, this has been lovely, but I must get back to Bobby's house." Claire stood readying to leave. Extending her hand to my friend, she offered Charlie an ingratiating smile designed to please.

"Claire, it was a pleasure meeting you, and possibly we may meet again. After all, we both live in the Bridgeton area. I'll make a point of looking you up when I get home."

"I'll look forward to seeing you again," she said smoothly.

"Claire, I mentioned breakfast in the morning; still interested?"

"I'd enjoy that, Dave, believe me."

I glanced at an expressionless Charlie. "Care to join us?"

His blank look turned to delight.

"You better believe it!"

I returned my eyes to Claire. "We'll pick you up at eight-thirty. How does that sound?"

"That sounds perfect."

She gave me Bobby's address, waved goodbye to Charlie, and then kissed me on the cheek. Turning, she headed for the sidewalk, glancing over her shoulder with a million-dollar smile.

Chapter 14

The sight of Claire sitting on Bobby's front porch surprised me. What's up with her? I wondered. She always made me wait when we dated, now she's checking her watch on the way to my vehicle. She stopped when Charlie jumped out of the Buick like a spring chicken.

"Hello again, you're right on time," he said, a broad grin plastered on his face. "How are you this fine morning?"

The pleased look on her face indicated she was intrigued by her unlikely suitor while Charlie scrambled to open the rear door.

"I feel much better after seeing you." Her reply carried with it a subtle subtext.

After settling in the back seat, I caught a glimpse of Claire primping in the rear view mirror.

Charlie turned to smile at me. "Dave, Christmas has come earlier than usual."

The sound of an astonished intake of breath, emanating from the backseat filled the car. Judging by my second glance, Claire appeared pleased by Charlie's comment.

After parking in the back lot of Betsy's Diner, Charlie once again scurried to open the door for his new acquaintance. I appraised Claire with an oblique look on our way to the diner.

She, unlike many women, has the looks accompanied by an aloofness that makes men light-headed. I couldn't help but smile.

Our waitress served us coffee and then took food orders. The aromas from the kitchen came before the food.

Charlie nervously rubbed his mouth. "Your friend from Casler is truly sensational." He spoke to me but raised his cup to Claire in salute.

She thanked him with a nod, color rising in her cheeks. Obviously Charlie's wild banter garnered her attention. It was evident in her eyes that she liked it.

After exchanging glances, their eyes momentarily fastened on each other, an unconcealed display of affection showing. They were communicating the old-fashioned way. Who was kidding whom? Their blatant reaction to each other in a brief matter of hours made me pause to marvel at how quickly the human psyche could recalibrate for its next challenge.

Charlie talked on, his words claiming Claire's undivided attention.

"Look what I brought you." Sally our waitress said as she approached our table.

Claire made a get-ready motion to Charlie, directing him to start eating.

She's just flirting and having fun just like she did in Casler. My observation caused me to smile.

Several minutes later, while spreading jam on a piece of toast, I accidentally dropped a touch on my hand. Standing up, I extended my hand to show the spot of preservative. "Excuse me, I have to hit the men's room and wash my hands."

After returning to the table, I felt left out listening to the two-way conversation, their rush of excitement all around me, but not meant for my ears. I did what came naturally and finished my hash and eggs in silence.

As they talked, I noticed Charlie shrug and smile. I felt saddened when Jane's face suddenly appeared in my mind. It had been three years since she passed away and I vowed that what was happening to Charlie wouldn't come around to me.

About the same time I was thinking of Jane, they whooped with laughter, reveling in their own world. He was pushing the edge of silliness to its limits.

"Charlie, you're acting like you stood in front of the *Mona Lisa* too long."

He let my remark slide while Claire gave me a curious look. Something unusual was in the offering; possibly a connection accompanied by some unmentionable activity. Now starts the fertility dance. It became obvious while watching her interact with Charlie that she was as proud, strong-willed, and determined as ever. My thought nudged me back to when she was wearing a purple and white Casler cheerleader's uniform. I missed much of their conversation, however, Charlie's voice stood out. "If you believe that, I know where there's a bridge for sale." Claire laughed while he rolled up his eyes at me. He was fast-approaching a foolish moment in his life that occasionally captures many men, and he didn't mind who knew it.

I almost fell on the floor when he said, "You're different than my wife, Betty."

Displaying considerable composure, Claire's sparkling eyes flickered in an understanding way. She sympathetically softened the impact of Charlie's faux pax by adeptly redirecting the exchange by saying to my friend, "It's going to be a lovely day." After a sip of coffee, she asked him, "Why did I bring that up?" There was no way Charlie could know the answer; a simple shrug was the only reply he could muster.

Moments passed before she laughed happily. "Now I remember. Let's do something different this afternoon."

After finishing breakfast, I talked about the Island Queen ferry ride to Martha's Vineyard and the wonders of the island. Claire, without comment, closed her eyes briefly, apparently in deep thought.

The minutes fell away to an hour of idle talk, after which I checked my watch. "We have time to catch the next ferry. Anyone interested?"

They looked at each other with eyes dancing an unspoken agreement.

"Sounds like a plan to me," she said, sounding like Claire Franklin of old. "What about it, Charlie?"

He appeared to be doing mental gymnastics while turning his cup around and around. "I'm your man," he said with a grin.

She set the hook with a final tug. "Wonderful! Let's get a move on," she said in an excited voice.

I had been reduced to a bystander, nothing more than a chauffeur. My instincts told me she had set her cap for Charlie, and my eyes assured me they were right. I liked what was happening around me, however, their attraction for each other caused me to think of Jane and how much I missed her.

On the short ride to the ferry, the thought hit me, that by accompanying them, I'd be in the way. Pulling up to the ferry drop off area, I pointed to the ship. "The harbor waters tell me you'll have a smooth ride to the island."

"You're not going?" Claire asked calmly.

Charlie, on the other hand, giggled like a teenager. Her presence was turning him into the Crown Prince of Foolishness. Following a difficult two years, I wondered how he thought of Betty now that Claire had entered the picture.

After leaving my vehicle, they headed for the ticket line when all at once he whirled around and spoke. "Wars are won or lost before they are fought."

"What the hell does that mean?" I asked with a puzzled smile.

"A foundation is laid before one constructs a building." With that said, Charlie turned to join Claire standing in the ticket line.

Not understanding his puzzling comment, I speculated that he was referring to his newfound connection with Claire. Still confused, I let it pass without a reply.

I guided my car into a ten-minute loading zone to watch the ferry leave. Holding hands at the bow, they waved goodbye.

"So long, pal, be good to her," I said in a whisper.

After the ferry pulled out, I headed back to the Heights, thinking on the way that Claire was playing for keeps, and had landed her catch of the day. All this in a twenty-four hour period, I marveled.

How Claire handled Charlie was an indecipherable verdict that could go either way. A sixth sense told me that with time, he might not be slipping into a binding relationship, but was making a convincing effort of working the edges.

Chapter 15

Falmouth seemed eerily quiet with small eddies of sand swirling to and fro across the beach. The Main Street fire station siren sounded, prompting me to check my watch. It read 6:15 AM, co-incidentally, the same time Claire Cummins pulled into my drive-way, the rear chock full of stuff.

She approached the porch with a business-like walk. I sensed before she announced her intentions that she was heading home. Claire stood in front of me nervously shuffling from foot to foot.

"It's been over two weeks since I last saw you, which caused me to worry," I said in a rushed voice.

"This isn't a social call. I couldn't slip away without saying goodbye. That's why I'm up so early," she said simply.

"I'm sorry to see you leave."

"Yes, well; it's something that has to be done."

A flock of geese appeared out of nowhere, their honks catch-ing our attention.

Disregarding the intrusion, Claire suddenly spoke, "Dave, I need some of your time."

"Certainly, what are friends for, if not for that?"

"I'm having trouble sorting out my thoughts," she said with a gentle grace, "maybe you can help me."

She needs a cup of coffee to settle down, I thought.

"Claire, excuse me while I get you a mug from the kitchen."

Several minutes after fixing her coffee, she settled down to talk.

"I truly enjoyed my stay in Falmouth, and I can't thank you enough for your hospitality. But there's something else." She bit down on her lip, waiting for me to speak. I let the moment play out by not breathing a word.

"I wanted Charlie to be the one from the first time we met. Everything fell into place for me, but he didn't. . ."

"If that's the case, let's talk about him."

"Both of us are carrying around a lot of baggage."

Tears suddenly raced down her cheeks. It was obvious she was under a great deal of stress. Even when distressed, she always displayed a dignity that I admired.

"Claire, everyone carries around a lot of baggage, but few talk about it."

"This has been a strange journey," she said.

"You've haven't talked about anything since arriving this morning. How about getting on with it and telling me of this strange journey of yours?"

My gentle reprimand startled her into pushing ahead.

"It's what I can give him. He's. . ." Claire didn't finish.

I pursued her thought. "Like what? What can you give him?"

"I can give him the companionship he's lacking. He brings out the best in me, and, believe me, that's hard work." She smiled at her attempt at humor. "Heartbreak is my hallmark. I have to get this right before I run out of time."

"What do you mean by 'get this right'? What are you talking about?"

Claire opened her hands to me in frustration.

"I don't know. The catch is, by some insane reason, Charlie really likes me." She shook her head in confusion.

"That sounds like a winning combination to me," I offered.

"I know, but ..." she paused to regroup. "Charlie rekindled my passion for life, and that scares me. This shouldn't have happened to me at my age, but it did."

"You have to understand he has a style all his own that seeps into his writing. Have you read any of his novels?"

"Not yet. Is he a creditable author?"

"Why would that concern you? He has more money than the bank downtown."

Tapping her fingers on the rocker arm, she glanced in my direction.

"It's not the money that concerns me; I have plenty of my own. There's something else. I feel emotionally exposed to feelings I don't understand."

"Did you talk last night?"

Claire sighed. "We did."

"Did you tell him about heading home?"

"Yes, yes," she said in a whisper. "The words I wanted to say to him failed me, and I stood looking at him like a dunce."

Her declaration caused me to laugh. "Claire, my dear, you're far from being a dunce. I know this first-hand."

Embarrassment tinted her smile. "Yes, that's a bit of a stretch, but you know what I mean."

I nodded in agreement, enjoying the sunny emotion she brought to her forced smile.

The haunting wail of a foghorn pierced the heavy air.

"That sound reminds me of home," Claire said with relish.

"We got sidetracked for a moment. Tell me what you have in mind."

"Charlie and I have a great deal in common, coming from the Bridgeton area and all."

"Small world, isn't it?"

"It is that. I desperately want to make this work, but. . ." her sentence trailed off. "Our friendship is like an itch that needs scratching, but I'm at a loss where to begin. For the life of me, I don't know what to do." She thrust her hands out in frustration once again, not speaking for moments on end until she blurted out, "Charlie asked me point-blank if I'd be interested in marrying him."

Now we're getting somewhere, I reminded myself. The haze is drifting away, leaving the nitty-gritty part of this romance in plain sight.

"It's none of my business, but what did you tell him?"

"I didn't have the heart to answer. My goodness, Dave, how can I marry a man I've known for less than three weeks? He means a great deal to me, but. . ."

"But that's the rub, you're not certain."

Dark clouds loaded with rain lurked overhead prompting me to think what lousy weather in which Claire had to drive home to Sands Beach.

She smiled at me but didn't answer.

Shrugging off her noncommittal attitude, I forged ahead.

"I suppose the appropriate question to ask is, "Are you serious about him?"

She bit down on her lip, lost in thought, searching for an answer.

That part of my Q & A strategy obviously failed, so I gave her my last parting shot. "Are you absolutely certain there is no other man you can love other than Charlie?"

She shrugged her shoulders as if to say the whole matter was beyond her.

"Claire, everyone lives with questions they can't answer, including you, including me. Think this over. What direction would you and I have taken if Charlie hadn't come along?" My stomach knotted up as I talked. "You know what the answer is, and please don't deny it. To save you the discomfort of admitting the truth, I'll fast forward to the future. If you don't understand where this is heading I'll spell it out for you. We probably would marry for no other reason than we were lonely. It's hard to compare love at eighteen with love at sixty-nine. However, our marriage would have taken a slide downhill to oblivion in the snap of your finger. Emotionally, it would be like were back in Casler as teenagers liking each other as friends, but not doing very well otherwise."

She looked solemn, a lone tear easing down her cheek.

"Don't think I haven't thought this over, because I have. Claire, much of your anxiety is self-imposed."

The lone tear on her cheek led to many. "How could you say that?"

"It was easy. You have options, you know."

She appeared to choose her words carefully.

"There's no need for further conversation concerning this matter at. . ." I tried to interrupt, but she curtly said, "Let me finish. At this point, our connection is just that, a connection with no bond." I sensed a hint of finality in her words.

"Does that little homily mean what I think it means?"

"Make whatever you want out of it!" Claire said, her one-sided reply honed with a sharp edge.

"I have a hypothetical situation for you to consider. If you and Charlie ever get together, will you be mean to him?"

"How could I possibly be mean to him when I love him so?" she said indignantly.

"Take this from your favorite dream-maker—the only thing you'll remember about Charlie is the good times you'll continue to have together, not the doubt you harbor now."

You and your memories, that's all I hear from you," she said.

"What you say is true, but I learn from them. Now let's get back to Claire Cummins. Your concerns lead me to believe you're afraid of this involvement with Charlie because your marriage failed, and you don't want that to happen again."

Claire shrugged.

"What you want and what you get may very well happen if you give it a chance. What happens, happens, that you can depend on. Let your heart be your guide, not your head."

Claire rose up from her chair. "I hate to leave Dave Foster, but my day needs restarting. It's been a delight seeing you again."

No sooner had she stood with her arm extended to shake hands than she sat down crying. Her tears seemed to flow endlessly until she finally gained control of herself.

"I was trying so hard to keep myself together, but look at me now," she said while wiping away the remaining tears. She rose again to say goodbye. The touch of her hand brought a new sensation with it. I had truly gained a friend for life. At that moment, a peace passed between us that we'd never known before.

"Your return home must be a two-day trip." She nodded. "Where will you stop tonight?"

"The drive to my daughter's home in Asbury Park, New Jersey will take roughly nine hours. I'll stay several days with Lucy, and then make the nine-hour trip home."

She looked away, signaling our talk had ended. I nodded, understanding her message.

A wisp of fog drifted unabated by the porch.

"It's the story of my life. I always seem to go half-way."

"What's your point?" I asked.

"Halfway means halfway. If you're not on line, I'll put you there. I have a proclivity for starting chores that eventually go unfinished."

Claire released me from her gaze, and then moved to her green van. Settling into the driver's seat, she rolled down the driver's side window. Placing my hands against the door, we talked through the window.

"You are an incredible lady," I said with meaning.

"Dave, you always know what to say." She then rewarded me with her million-dollar smile.

"I'll worry about you until you call from your home."

"That's sweet and thank you for your concern," again flashed her brilliant smile.

"Be careful and have a safe trip," I counseled.

"I shall, and let's do it again sometime." Her sweet voice reminded me of two kids at a junior prom in Casler.

Claire suddenly got out of the van and, much to my surprise hugged and kissed me warmly. Returning to the controls, she started the vehicle and said, in barely a whisper, "Dave, think good thoughts of me."

She put the van in gear. Slowly pulling away, she left me with a dispirited wave. In the space of less than a minute, Claire had driven out of sight.

I took a last look down Grand Avenue and thought, what could have been? Sighing audibly, I returned to my porch with an empty feeling, knowing full-well that the remainder of the day would prove bittersweet.

Chapter 16

The screaming sun, unmercifully beating on the Heights, drove me from the bench I occupied to the relative comfort of the porch. Clear air carrying a crisp scent of sea salt helped neutralize the heat.

It had been close to three weeks since last seeing Charlie, and now here he was on my porch displaying a troubled countenance. Bright sunlight had caused perspiration to sparkle beneath his closely-cropped brush-cut.

"I figured you ran away," I smiled.

Shaking his head, he answered, "No, nothing like that. I've been with Claire all the time, and would like your advice."

"Fire away. What's this all about?"

He appeared to shift his thoughts around before speaking.

"Looking hard at my situation, I believe there's woman trouble in the future for me," he declared, sweeping his hand forward in an anxious gesture.

You may be a little long in the tooth for that, I thought.

"This has something to do with Claire, doesn't it?"

"It does."

"Let's kick it around," I proposed.

Apparently accepting my suggestion, he started his discourse cautiously, not rushing.

Looking eye to eye, he grinned. "You were right about being obsessed with a ghost; I was. Interestingly enough, maybe there's a story about that ghost now that she's flesh and blood. I haven't been around her long enough to really get to know her, but enough to experience her warmth and goodness. Claire gives me a gentle calm when I'm near her."

He grinned happily. "Open an onion and you'll find many layers. She's like that onion, something new every day. When I was with her, my heart pounded so hard I could hardly catch my breath. Dave, maybe I fell in love with her and didn't know it."

"That's a little of a stretch, Charlie, but I'll give you a pass on it."

"She doesn't look her age," he offered.

"Yes, I know."

"Claire and I liked each other immediately after we met. She's special, and I'm not looking through rose-colored glasses when I say that." He looked at the beach for several moments before returning his eyes to me. "You know, Dave, I've considered calling her a poster woman with an attitude."

"If you ever use that description to her face, she'd soundly kick you flat in the ass." We both laughed at my feeble attempt at humor.

"It felt natural when we were together, but now that's she's home, I feel lousy and lonely. I've been going it alone since Betty died, never filling the vacancy she left." Dropping his head in a hopeless manner, he began talking to the floor. "I'd grown used to being alone. In other words, old Charlie had been out of touch. Then I met Claire on your porch," he waved his hand around, "and life hasn't been the same since. I worry whether I'm ready to make any further commitment."

"Get a grip on yourself and flow with the current. Charlie, it's the way of the world, and there's nothing you can do about it."

"Your moralizing discourse isn't making it!"

"I'm just trying to break your funk. You've been talking trash since you got here, but haven't revealed one iota about you and Claire."

He exhaled in complete frustration. "Since we first met, I've quizzed you about your Casler history. Claire Franklin's name settled loud and clear in my mind to the point, it nearly drove me crazy."

"Don't take this personally, but I'm curious. I've not seen you two for close to three weeks. What have you been up to?"

He smiled. "I got into a different program."

My puzzled look made him laugh.

Not understanding his comment, I speculated that he was referring to his newfound connection with Claire. Still confused, I let it pass without a reply.

"It became evident we had a great deal in common."

"Like what?"

"One day we walked by an array of multi-colored summer flowers in front of the big library downtown, and enjoyed them so much we sat on a bench admiring them for a lengthy time. We drifted to several locations on the beach and just watched the water. We took in several movies, a couple of Commodores' games, and hit the restaurant scene practically ever night. How's that for being busy?"

"You're right. You two have a lot in common."

"I believed everything had fallen in place for Claire and the Lone Warrior. What an experience!"

I raised my eyebrows, "Everything?"

He moved his hand up and down. "I'd say that pretty much covers it."

Charlie is giving me a different take on how he feels, I thought.

"I sense you have more to tell me," I suggested.

"Claire told me not to get in touch with her for a month. She explained her reasoning which prompted me to ask her why. 'Time was important to get her ducks in order if she was going to settle down' was her answer."

I listened intently. "So, you're under orders?"

He nodded his agreement. "I've been having a difficult time getting my mind around what she said."

"Sounds like a good idea to me. Just remember, Noah built the Ark before it started to rain," I advised.

"I'm missing what you're saying," Charlie said with a puzzled frown.

"This is straight up and down. Are you up to the mark?"

"It never occurred to me that I wasn't," he said indignantly. "She's in my best interest."

"Romance has its pitfalls," I counseled, and then asked, "what if it doesn't work out?"

His face registered a pained grimace.

Quick to reply, he asked with urgency creeping into his voice, "What have I lost if it doesn't?"

His was a question I cared not answer.

"Dave, I'm a caricature of an old guy who doesn't know what in the hell he's doing and senses the chance of a lifetime slipping away."

"You're reading too much into this. Do you remember me telling you about coming home from the school picnic after Claire dumped me? I told Dad what happened, causing him to give me advice I've never forgotten. 'Never confuse what you know with what you think you know.' Anything in that humble little homily you can use?"

"Yes, I believe there is. Hopefully, something will come up that works."

"I don't doubt that it will, and good luck with whatever passes between you and Claire in the future."

"Thank you, Dave, I didn't need a reason to see you other than to say goodbye," Charlie said, displaying a broad smile. "Well, maybe I also had Claire on my mind."

"When you mentioned Claire, this thought came to mind. A good companion brings good luck and happiness. She will be that good companion, trust me."

"I hope so."

"If anything comes up, you can reach me at my home address in Portland. You have my card?"

He nodded yes. "It's been a treat knowing you, Dave."

"I'll never forget you. Keep in touch, my friend, and write a great love story. After your Falmouth visit, I imagine you know all about that stuff."

He smiled. "I plan to do just that, and I learned much of it from you."

While wishing him a safe trip home, he shook my hand. "Goodbye, old pioneer, and remember to hang in there while keeping your powder dry."

With that, Charlie Jamison, aka Justin Astor, left the porch, and continued walking down Worchester Court, never to look back.

Chapter 17

After finishing the obligatory task of closing up the Falmouth house for the winter, I felt exhausted and not quite up to par. The thought that I was coming down with the flu crossed my mind. I also considered it might be the emotion of seeing Claire and Charlie leaving for Virginia that drained me, possibly a combination of both. Whatever the reason, I decided that going to bed for a lengthy sleep would renew my energy for the next day's drive home.

My rest was not as planned. I was up and down, walking around the house when awake, pitching and tossing masquerading as sleeping when in bed. I awoke early in the morning with a start. The dream I experienced was stark and distinctive, calling to mind a friend in Portland who can recall each of his dreams in their entirety including color, sound, dialogue, themes and character descriptions.

If I have a dream, it's well on the way to being forgotten by the time I'm fully awake. Occasionally, parts remain, but these occasions are few and far between. This dream was different though; I remembered all of it. Catherine Hislop was featured. Not the pitiful edition from my early days in Casler, rather the mature twenty-four year old woman I met in Woolworth's.

The image had a touch of gray nestled in a mass of straw-colored hair accompanied by flawless skin with hardly a wrinkle. Tall and erect, Catherine was dressed to kill—down to her knees. Without stockings, her footwear was a dead give away that this was an unusual dream with no obvious meaning. The vague apparition was wearing the same scruffy shoes with twine laces that she wore as a kid.

My fantasy started to fade when Catherine said, "Hello, David, it's nice to see you again." It ended when she reached down to keep her skirt from blowing around, exposing her boil-covered legs.

I usually return to the Cape in October to check the house, but when I turned the key locking the front door, that final gesture ended another summer/fall season at Falmouth Heights. This five-month retreat to Cape Cod had been different from any I had ever experienced before.

When I crossed the Sagamore Bridge, driving northbound to Portland, for no good reason, my mind started working overtime, bringing up thoughts that intrigued me. The last few weeks at the Heights had been refreshing, even more than that, exciting. First, I met Charlie Jamison, in so many ways a man like myself. The one glaring difference being I was retired while he still worked as an accomplished author. And then Claire Franklin Cummins, a girlfriend from my high school days whom I'd not seen in over fifty years, entered my sheltered life.

Not knowing each other prior to meeting on my porch, they came together as if their chance meeting had been preordained by a higher power. All the time their nascent romance blossomed, I sat back in a state of confusion and watched it thrive. Here they were, in my backyard, working their way through unrelenting obstacles that complicate old age. Their endeavors caused me to marvel at their determination to start life anew. Now they had left Falmouth to return to their respective Virginia homes. As for me, I'm leaving the Heights by myself, richer for having started a new friendship and rekindled another.

Traffic picked up considerably when I approached the Braintree area. At that time, my thoughts drifted to my earlier dream. The reverie haunted me, but I wasn't going to be another Charlie and worship a ghost. Try as I might not to go back in time, thoughts of Catherine in Mrs. Warner's sixth grade class returned. I barely remember her other than those beat-up shoes and twine laces. The boils on her legs, however, were more than sketchy images, they were indelible truths engraved on my mind forever.

I tried hard to wipe the thought of that poor soul from my mind. Try as I might, her image kept bouncing around in my mind, followed by a torrent of questions: Was she alive? If so, where did she live? Was she married? Did she have children? My questions started running into each other, leaving me confounded.

At times my mind worked as if in a vacuum, and that's where it rested when crossing into Maine from New Hampshire. I found myself searching for answers to the same questions that dogged me Boston to Maine. My compulsion to seek Catherine out was rapidly becoming a obsession by the time I pulled into the driveway of my Portland home.

So overwhelmed by the desire to discover something about her, I sat in my car thinking about why I needed to know. My focus switched to Charlie and his admitted attraction to a ghost named Claire Franklin. I had become more like Charlie with each mile traveled between Braintree and Portland.

While setting my house in order for winter, I found myself thinking of hiring a private investigator; fortunately, that idea quickly faded. At that moment, her older sister popped into my mind, prompting me to recall going to Woolworth's to see Dorothy and meeting Catherine before leaving for graduate school in North Carolina. Dorothy had worked at the lunch counter during the day and attended night school to gain her degree and teacher certification. If Dorothy had worked as a teacher, she would have long since retired; so, where would I begin? I knew where to go if she had worked in the Portland system. I called a friend who had retired from the Portland Board of Education, asking him to search for Dorothy.

Two hours later he called me with her address and phone number.

Much to my surprise, she remembered me when I called. We talked several minutes before she agreed to meet me downtown for lunch the next day.

Seeing Dorothy again took me back to our brief talk at the lunch counter years ago. When I talked of my adult working years in Portland, she surprised me by knowing of my coaching career at Potham.

As Dorothy updated her story, I remembered her more than I did Catherine. Although she was four years older than I, it was her difficult and outspoken ways that stood out for me as a kid. The time had come to ask about Catherine.

Dorothy told me about Catherine's final three years in Orino, and her decision to move to the Portland area. She left it at that. We sat in silence while Dorothy considered my request to know where Catherine lived. She looked at me as if guarding a national security secret.

Don't do this to me, I thought. She relented by giving me what I needed to contact her sister.

While we said our goodbyes, a knowing smile settled on her face when she told me we'd be seeing each other in the near future.

Her farewell puzzled me, but I came away with a nice lunch of fried clams and, better yet, Catherine's address and phone number.

An unanticipated thought crossed my mind that she might find an excuse not to go out with me. I went through a brief period of having second thoughts about calling her, causing my nerves to seize up the way they used to before the start of a game. "Let's get on with it," I told myself, while reaching for the phone.

Her voice sent a chill through me. It was good to hear her speak. We entered into a benign conversation for several minutes before I asked her if she'd do me a favor. Her answer surprised me when she said it depended on the favor. There was nothing left to say other than asking the question on the tip of my tongue, and that was if she'd do me the honor of going to dinner with me. She grew silent, seemingly lost in thought. Prompted by her reticence, I impulsively suggested it was only a dinner invitation, nothing more. She sounded less than enthusiastic when she answered, but at least she accepted my request.

Our conversation ended with plans for a dinner date the following evening.

Chapter 18

This is about the life and times of an older Catherine Hislop. I was fast-approaching the truth about whether I was emotionally ready to begin dating after being without Jane for three years.

Nagging, unclear thoughts crowded my mind as I approached her house, and then they came to me. Had I been too impetuous and acted with my heart instead of my mind? Would meeting her reveal we had nothing in common, and resulting in an ill-advised romance? I pondered these doubts while ringing the door bell.

After opening the door, Catherine silently stood looking at me, a captivating smile crossing her face. At that moment, two seventy-year old senior citizens prepared to race back in time. I thought her striking as opposed to beautiful, with a classy image complementing her crisp appearance. Hints of gray streaking her once-blonde hair framed an unblemished face that displayed a complexion clear as Waterford glass with hardly a wrinkle; she had aged well. Color shaded her face while her brown eyes scanned my face. Her intake of breath was barely audible.

Looking at her made me feel twelve years old again. What we experienced at that moment was no commonplace event.

She pressed her hand forward in a surprisingly firm hand-shake. I nervously gave her a crooked smile after anxiously clearing my throat.

"Hello, Catherine. The years have been kind to you."

She returned my greeting with a voice hardly above a whisper. "Hello, David, it's nice to see you again. The last time we met was at Woolworth's before you headed for graduate school in North Carolina."

"I'm pleased you remember, and to be exact, it was forty-six years back."

Images of an unsmiling little girl with boils pushed into my thoughts. That memory was like a ghost that was always around.

"I have to thank you for calling," she said with a soft voice. "It's been so long," her voice trailed off. Changing her line of thinking, she asked, "How long have you known that I live in Casler?"

"I talked to Dorothy."

"Dear Dorothy, she's been the family matriarch since mother and dad passed away. Where are my manners? Please come in."

She led me into a tastefully appointed living room that could easily grace the cover of *Better Homes and Gardens* magazine. The forced talk that continued over the next fifteen minutes made me feel uncomfortable.

"I made a reservation at The Boathouse for eight o'clock. We can take our time and leisurely walk if you like."

She approved my suggestion with a nod. "Yes, that would be nice."

Catherine walked with a graceful ease, courtly with every step. I felt we were living the American dream as we walked along a street lined with sugar maple trees.

The full moon's rays drifting through multi-colored leaves waiting to fall created mottled shadows on the ground. Combined with light from old-fashioned street lamps, the confluence created an atmosphere that took on an amber tone.

Approaching the front entrance of the restaurant, I took hold of her elbow to serve as a guide through the glass door entrance. Touching her brought about a strange sensation, one I was unfamiliar with. Entering the building brought back memories of Jane. This treasure of a restaurant had been her favorite, and I had grown to love it as well. We had enjoyed birthdays, anniversaries, holidays, first-time-out dinners for each of the kids, quiet dinners for the two of us, and no other reason than to have a good meal. I hadn't returned to the restaurant since Jane's tragic death, and immediately felt a touch of guilt for bringing another woman to Jane's favorite eatery.

Judging by her surprised look, I guessed this was Catherine's first visit to The Boathouse.

"Oh, my," she said, displaying a smile that caused women her age to like her and men to think her pretty.

We entered a large dining room with a motif highlighted in Nantucket blue from carpet to perfectly folded napkins on white tablecloths. Blood-red china added an appealing touch to the room. The headwaiter placed us at a lakeside table next to floor-to-ceiling windows that ran the length of the room.

I noticed Catherine look around as if on a treasure hunt, finally resting her eyes on Casler Lake. The full-blown moon hanging in the sky created a golden path across the dark lake water that seemingly directed its rays to our table. I then became aware that her gaze was tracking the golden pathway to its source.

"A penny for your thoughts?" I asked.

"What we're seeing can't be bottled. This view takes my breath away," she said with an engaging smile.

As time passed by, we sat in silence studying the scene playing out in front of us. A feeling of contentment I'd not experienced since Jane died settled over me while I obliquely stole a glance at Catherine. Caught in the act, she smiled while turning to face me, her mature good looks on display.

"Catherine, you're pretty as a picture." My compliment sounded corny when it came out, causing me to ask myself why I said it.

"Thank you for that," she said with a embarrassed smile.

Our waitress interrupted the nice tempo of our conversation when she served our drinks, a white wine for her, a bottle of beer for me.

"We're not kids anymore," she whispered.

"I know, but certain things in life don't change," I said. Why did I say that? I thought while questioning the meaning of my words.

"I know about your coaching career, but little else. Would you fill in the gaps that I'm lacking?"

I spoke of my undergraduate days at Potham, my service time, and then followed with my experience at the University of North Carolina as a football graduate assistant. I then recounted meeting Jane, and the courtship that followed. My narrative continued with our graduation from graduate school, marriage, and a move back to Portland. I spoke of the most important part of my life— Jane and the three children. Finally, I forced myself to mention the void that was left after Jane's untimely death.

"It's been three years since she passed away. I should be over it by now, but I'm not. Her influence will always mark my way."

Catherine's gaze drifted past me, soon to return to make eye contact.

"Your Jane must have been special. I feel sorrow for your great loss," she said with misty eyes.

"You can't imagine what a comfort it is to hear you say that."

At that moment our food was served. During dinner, we talked about our children instead of ourselves. There was more to talk about than time would allow. We found that talking about her four and my three kept us busy.

During our leisurely walk to her home, Catherine asked if I'd like a home-cooked meal and I readily accepted. Our date ended with a handshake.

Thoughts about the protocol of dating for seniors kept running through my mind on the thirty-minute drive back to Portland. The puzzling portion of my evening with Catherine kept running through my mind. I was expecting a rather dull night with little to talk about, but surprisingly, our conversation easily flowed about a variety of topics. As I replayed our night's conversation, the thought came to mind that I had talked like a teenager on his first date. There were several possibilities why I had acted so dimwitted. One, I was nervous; two, I was out of practice.

Eventually my musings produced a solid conclusion. My feelings of having a pleasant evening made me feel young again. On the other hand, the guilt that had consumed me was the result of my anxiety. I liked being with her, but I was still missing Jane.

Chapter 19

Catherine mentioned dinner would be served at seven o'clock, compelling me to arrive early as a courtesy to my hostess. She motioned me to the table promptly at seven and then served an ordinary garden salad. The main course, a deep brown beef stew dished out in large pasta bowls followed. Piping-hot dinner rolls from the oven lifted the meal above the commonplace. As if her dinner wasn't enough, she served a generous piece of butterscotch meringue pie to conclude the meal.

Pushing back from the table to enjoy coffee, my too-full stomach indicated I had over eaten. The food was so tasty and basic in composition, I couldn't help myself. Catherine had turned her efforts into an elegant dinner.

After clearing the dinner dishes, we retreated to the front porch where I talked at length about what a superb cook she was.

At some point the conversation rolled around to our favorite songs when we were young. Catherine asked, "Do you remember the song, 'I Can Dream Can't I?'"

"Now that you mention it, I do."

The start of a smile settled on her lips. "Suddenly you've entered my life and the past days in Casler are slipping back into my mind. Certainly you can remember how poor we were. The most prized possession we owned was an old-fashioned Victrola that had to be cranked to work. You turned the handle on the side until it got tight, then you could play a 78 rpm record." Catherine laughed at the memory.

Memories she'd secretly hidden for any number of reasons surfaced. "Mother and dad had records from when they were first married and we played them constantly. After the bad times hit, they never bought another record."

She paused to sip her wine.

Where is she going with this story? I thought while waiting for her to resume.

"One day while walking home from school, I looked down and spotted a fifty-cent piece on the sidewalk. It was the first money I can ever remember having. To me, possessing that coin meant having a fortune in my hands and I wasn't going to tell anyone of my discovery. My kids used to say that money burned a hole in my pocket." Catherine appeared pleased with her anecdote. "I spent several weeks agonizing over what to buy, but couldn't decide. One day after school, I was listening to our new table Philco radio, well ... it wasn't new. Dad had chopped some wood for a neighbor and she paid him with a radio that didn't work. He was good at fixing things and somehow got the radio working. One day I was playing it when "I Can Dream, Can't I?" came on. The words and music made me think of you." Even though her face took on a embarrassed look, her spirit and voice continued to grow with excitement. "Now I knew what to buy. Going into Fuller's 5 & 10 was a first for me. I bought the record for forty-nine cents and got a penny in change. Mother was furious when she found out what I'd done and reminded me that so much could be done with fifty cents. When my father heard about my stunt, I expected him to have a fit, but his fit never came. It never occurred to me what I had done until he explained mother's reaction.

"As I look back, it was a selfish gesture on my part, but you must understand it was the first new thing I'd ever owned." She shook her head in wonder. "Can you imagine living like that as a kid? When I told my children that story, they found it hard to believe we lived like that. Several days later all had been forgotten and that song could be heard around the house night and day for weeks." She smiled shyly in my direction.

Catherine stood up and walked to a stereo cabinet in the living room, bending on one knee, in a sensual way that appeared unintended, to retrieve a 78 rpm record album. Returning to her chair, she pulled out a black record.

I had no idea what she had in mind when she gingerly passed me the black disc with a half-embarrassed look. She carefully held it by its edge while looking down at the sixty-year old relic. Even though it was battered and scratched, I could discern the printing on the label, "I Can Dream, Can't I?," with the artist's name, Jo Stafford, included underneath.

We talked on, pretty much covering the popular music of our youth until I changed the subject.

"How did it happen that your family recovered from this mess called the Depression?" I asked.

"How did it happen, you ask? That's a very easy question to answer. Good fortune finally embraced the Hislop family when Dad settled into his job in Farmington. Our family's lifestyle changed dramatically. For the first time that I can remember, we had money for store-bought goods. Our fortunes turned around. My parents saved enough money to buy an old rambling house in town, sizable enough to accommodate our large family.

"You'll remember this, I'm sure. The nation was fighting a two-ocean war, so young men found themselves in the service. Dad was too old to be drafted; he had served in World War I."

While Catherine talked I listened intently.

Catherine laughed. "When we first moved up there, the family was like a fish out of water. Everything in our life changed. You may find this hard to believe, but it was the first time we experienced indoor plumbing. Our coal was delivered by truck and dumped down a chute next to the furnace, unlike the days when we picked up loose coal along the railroad tracks. And, to top it off, Dad bought a used black 1936 two-door Plymouth."

"You brought me back to my youth in a hurry when you mentioned coal being delivered to the basement. Another memory you mentioned caught my attention. Dad had a black Ford. I can't remember many cars that weren't painted black back then. Once your family had a car, I imagine you drove around the state to see the sights."

"Not really. Back then, there was gas rationing and, because Dad walked to work, we only qualified for the minimum ration of gas. You've forgotten about the black "A" sticker placed on the windshields, haven't you?"

Her smile turned into a happy laugh. It was fun being around her when she displayed her contented feelings, which was often.

"I came of age in Upstate Maine and loved everything about it, still do as a matter-of-fact. The seasons were wonderful and distinctive, my favorite being fall. Up there, the season flowed around you like a gentle breeze."

"And then winter came, you neglected to mention that," I reminded her.

"For good reason," she said with a smile. "The season rests on the area like a flatiron. I recall the economy was bleak, but showing signs of improving. Two different lifestyles existed side by side in town. The people who worked at the college and the mill where Dad worked weren't living comfortably, but getting by, while the rest of the community faced hard times."

"You didn't mention the rich families in Farmington," I advised.

Catherine laughed shallowly. "The rich are like mosquitoes in summer, they're always around."

"Farmington sounds a little like Casler did back then," I pointed out.

Catherine nodded. "Very much the same, except we had a college."

"Is that the school you attended?"

"Yes. Farmington State was a jewel in a threadbare town and it served us well. It was a teachers' college back then, offering elementary teacher certification and library science, which was my major. Farmington wasn't for everyone, just those planning to teach.

"I lived home and rode my bike to school. Working part time at both the village and college library kept me busy and I loved every minute of it. Classes were a breeze for me, so I never spent much time studying.

"Tuition was an incredibly low fifty dollars a semester. I made enough to pay for tuition, books, clothes, and even had a little left over for spending money."

"It sounds as if you had things coming your way," I said with admiration.

"I did, and it got better," she said with a broad smile.

The thought suddenly came to me that she had a brilliant smile, hard to forget. As bright as it was, however, it was not as sensational as Claire Cummins' smile. After all, Claire had the most astonishing smile of any woman found on this earth.

"In my junior year I needed a history course to fulfill a core requirement, so I chose 'History of Colonial Maine.'"

Catherine moistened her lips and smiled.

"Frank Cooper was a teaching assistant who taught the class. He didn't hold my attention in one way or the other for much of the semester. I had watched him from a distance and found him nice-looking as opposed to handsome. One day in class Frank made a remark about how the Pilgrims should have burned the virgins at the stake instead of making history the way they did. That comment brought the house down with laughter, causing me to take a closer look at him. Instead of seeing him as a no-nonsense man where casual talk was difficult, I realized he was a model of propriety with an orderly, curious mind. Frank's gentle manner commanded respect while revealing that teaching was his gift. Among other things, he displayed a brilliant sense of humor that would help propel him on a fast track to success."

"He sounds like someone I would like."

"You would, David. I can visualize you and Frank sitting on our front porch in Orono enjoying each other's company while savoring a beer." She made a happy laugh that compelled me to join her.

"Somehow he asked me out. From that first date, it seemed as if we were on the same page. I fell head over heels for him. What followed was your typical girl-meets-boy scenario. The next thing I knew, he proposed to me and we married the summer before my senior year. Who would have believed it, your classmate at Casler with boils on her legs, owning a single dilapidated dress and shoddy shoes had married the prize of a lifetime? Do you remember the 1980 Olympic hockey game against the Russians? The American team was leading with seconds to go when Al Michaels said to the TV audience, 'Do you believe in miracles?' Talk about miracles, I had myself a college professor."

Chapter 20

"Catherine, I ate so much, a nice walk might be in order, even a visit to The Boathouse if you'd like."

"Yes, I'd like that."

Our casual stroll resembled last night's with one prominent difference. I did much of the talking on our first date while Catherine claimed center stage on the second night.

We settled at the bar instead of the dining room. After the drinks arrived, I asked her to continue.

"You left off where you married the professor," I reminded her.

A soft smile rested on her face as she looked back to earlier days in Farmington. "I moved into his apartment in town. It was clean, orderly, and eclectic in nature, more a man's way station, than anything else. I immediately set out decorating and adding a woman's touch to the rooms.

"Frank was nearing completion of his PhD in History at the University of Maine, which forced him to drive eighty miles to Orono and back twice a week. His hectic life was of his own making, but he continually displayed an unflappable enthusiasm while completing his studies. I am proud to say he became a poster boy for success. While he was immersed in a mad dash to finish his studies, I busied myself buying used furniture."

Catherine laughed. "It was like going on a treasure hunt. My mother called me a 'black belt shopper' because I could always search out quality pieces at the lowest prices. Furnishing the apartment proved to be an ongoing work in progress. I bought old pieces that, when refinished, proved to be valuable. The collection of hand-me-downs was varied, but became my pride and joy. In fact, my house is still furnished with some of them. My father taught me how to refinish furniture, which later became a

hobby I enjoy to this day. Have you ever refinished furniture?"
She asked.

"Not really. To be honest, I wouldn't know where to begin."

"It's not that hard. You clean the old surface with paint stripper, clean and sand the exposed wood, and then apply a mixture of linseed oil and turpentine," she smiled, "and a lot of elbow grease."

I laughed at her enthusiasm. "I'm glad you cleared that up for me. What happened then?"

She smiled at my question. "Now comes the fun part. The following June I graduated from Farmington. Two weeks later Frank was awarded his PhD. Talk about miracles, the first came our way when he was awarded a position as an assistant professor of History at the University of Maine. Two weeks after that, miracle number two came our way; we relocated to Orono where we purchased a big, old-fashioned house with a sweeping wraparound front porch in a charming neighborhood near the university. The area was hardly high-end, however we had nice neighbors and it suited us nicely."

I liked the ease with which she talked, almost like a woman totally in tune with what she had accomplished in life.

"We spent considerable time on the porch, sometimes talking about little or nothing. In front of our house was an old-time cobbled street. That road of stones added a special luster to the neighborhood and I loved every stone in that bumpy old avenue.

"My own advanced education life was taking on a life of its own. After arriving in Orono, I started working on my master's degree and finished in a year. Not to be forgotten, of course, was Frank. My earlier assessment of him had been on target. He quickly became a very popular figure on campus. I think the city and the university were the centerpiece of his and my existence."

"You must have had a pleasant experience living up there. It sounds as if life has been kind to you."

Catherine nodded her head in agreement. "We practiced an Alice-in-Wonderland approach to life, you know, let tomorrow be your future. As the years rolled by, our station in life continued to improve.

"Astonishingly, Frank became Dean of the College of Liberal Arts and I was appointed head librarian of the university library.

During that span of time, I had acquired a PhD, and raised four children." Catherine laughed at herself. When the weather was good, it seemed, I had babies in a playpen on the porch for years.

"During that period, Frank mastered the art of brewing his own beer and had bottle labels printed that just delighted him to no end."

She handed me a sealed label withdrawn from her purse. It read,

Black Bear Lager

When a Person Tires of Beer

They Tire of Life

Brewed in Orono, Maine

by Frank Cooper

"This label is incredible. Did your husband brew much beer?"

"He brewed it by the gallons. In fact, ten cases at a time."

"How could he drink all that beer?" I asked with obvious astonishment.

"He didn't, silly." Her laugh attracted interest from others sitting at the bar. It was fun being with her I thought, just to hear her happy laugh was good enough for me.

"He might drink a beer at supper and that would be it for the day. Frank was a taster, not a drinker. He bought every brand available and tasted it. One of his goals in life was to design the ultimate beer. David, he gave away most of the beer he made or bought.

"Years later, I sensed something was different with Frank, but foolishly turned a blind eye to those observations. I hoped whatever it was would go away, but finally realized something unusual was happening with his physical health. He occasionally would bump into a piece of furniture or knock over a glass or dish at the dinner table. It became apparent he was losing some dexterity, but not an alarming degree. The physical work he normally did in the garden suddenly depleted his energy, causing him to tire easily.

"One night, while tending his vegetables, he reached for a nearby hoe, lost his balance, and fell. I witnessed the incident and immediately realized he needed medical attention. After a cursory examination, our family doctor referred Frank to a neurologist. After a series of tests, Dr. LePoint personally called to arrange a meeting the following day"

I didn't care for the direction her story was taking, but continued to listen intently.

"The next day we sat in his office anxiously waiting for Dr. LePoint. He finally arrived and immediately shook our hands. Finally settled behind his desk, he nervously cleared his throat. His words are indelibly lodged in my mind; I guess they always will be. He said with considerable difficulty, 'There is no possible way other than to tell the truth. Frank, you have just been diagnosed with Lou Gehrig's disease.' "

Maybe Catherine's retelling of her husband's physical demise dampened the moment, causing her to suggest leaving. We left the restaurant after finishing our drinks to return to the comfort of her porch. I think though it was never mentioned that we both felt the magic of last night's dinner had faded. We didn't talk on the return, but I sensed time would be a factor before she finished talking about Frank.

We sat for a long while without talking before Catherine continued.

"David, my well-ordered world was rapidly becoming unmanageable. Dr. LePoint was delicately up front with us the way he talked.

"He told us Frank's illness could be partially treated with a regimen of medicine he proposed. Dr. LePoint talked about the issues that would come up, such as a progressive decline of his muscular structure and organ functions. His final pronouncement practically floored me: he told us there was a multitude of pieces of his bodily functions waiting to go wrong.

"As we were confronted with his prognosis, doubts surfaced whether I was strong enough to face each new day. The doctor asked Frank if he had any questions." Catherine's eyes filled with tears before she continued. "Frank asked him point-blank how much time he had. I'll never forget how Dr. LePoint reacted: he didn't speak for a long moment before pushing his hands out in front of him. He told us, probably within a year but had no way of knowing; the decision was in the hands of a higher power. David, up to that moment, I realized I had misjudged Frank's situation, but the harsh reality of Dr. LePoint's explanation forced me to realize my husband of so many years was going to die.

"Days turned into months, but the fight for his life wasn't over; Frank kept hammering away. First, he retired from the university, and then he started setting his affairs in order every waking hour of the day. Over the years, to no avail, a large Milwaukee brewery had tried to buy his beer recipe. Although severely ill, he drove a hard bargain, and, when finally persuaded to sell, he commanded a startling amount of money." Catherine bit down on her lip as tears flowed down her face.

Watching her suffer caused my mind to skip back to a sixth grader by the name of Catherine Hislop who displayed enormous mental strength and resiliency. Fighting to finish what she started, she wiped her tears away with a tissue.

I wondered if she was as strong now as back then.

"I witnessed the rapid deterioration of a robust man. His once-thick hair was showing signs of scalp. The shadow of death loomed in his eyes. But Frank didn't go easily. In my heart, I believe he realized his time had come. This may sound odd, but I'm certain he passed away with dignity." Her eyes shined with tears.

Her series of flashbacks caused my heart to ache for her loss.

"On balance, ours was a good marriage. It seemed Frank's fingerprints could be found anywhere you looked in the North Country. His absence left a void I've never filled." Catherine laughed. "Frank constantly used the expression, 'twisting in the wind,' and that's where he left me. A loved one's death has a way of sneaking up on a person, as you well know."

"Catherine, I fully understand how difficult it is for you to talk about your husband's death."

She smiled. "David, I don't leave loose ends unfinished after starting something. Maybe it's part of my DNA."

How unlike Claire's half-way attitude, I thought to myself.

"There's another thing that needs saying. Other than Dorothy, you're the first person I've talked to about Frank's illness. David, I've trusted you since our brief time together in sixth grade. It's important to me that you feel my pain and enjoy my happy moments."

Her thought about painful and happy moments left me puzzled. Understanding her need to finish, I proposed, "I'd like to hear the rest."

Catherine nodded as if she'd read my mind.

"In a far corner of my mind, I realized I had to get control of my life because I wasn't making the most of a difficult situation," she explained matter-of-factly. Months later my life changed dramatically when I learned how to handle the storm. Dorothy made me realize that blood is thicker than water and I should follow her lead. She convinced me, after numerous hours of debate, that I should break with the past and move to the Portland area.

"Dorothy pointed out that life had a way of working out and a sudden change of location would be a litmus test of my character. By my own definition of change, I didn't intend to reinvent myself, but it didn't work that way. One should never look back, but I did. Thoughts of my youth in Casler, however abbreviated, entered my mind and I went where my heart led me." Catherine shrugged.

"When I bought the house here in Casler, the porch we're sitting on was the major attraction. It has proven very therapeutic." She rubbed her eyes with the backs of her fingers.

"And there you have it, my chapter and verse."

A woman's Horatio Alger story, I thought.

Chapter 21

The letter postmarked "Bridgeton, VA" arrived at my Portland home on Halloween. I hastily opened the envelope anticipating Charlie's news.

Dave,

I'm from the old school and refuse to use email, thus the handwritten communiqué. Here I am in Bridgeton settled in for the next phase of my life.

My cry for help was answered during my stay in Falmouth. I'd been out of touch with the world, withdrawn and existing in a wasteland known as depression. Constant thoughts of Betty never left me. Those memories were enough to sustain me through a difficult period that followed her death, but I understand there has to be more to life than memories.

You undoubtedly are aware we both have been tarred with the same brush. After our fortuitous meeting, followed by considerable bench talk, I came to marvel at how you managed your own grief. Your example made me gradually understand that my life was not as it seemed, and going it alone didn't make much sense. I had to have a reason for going on. I realized a man must play the cards dealt him, but didn't know how to go about it.

The haze I was living through dramatically lifted when I met Claire on your porch. How it happened is a mystery to me, but sheer chance had to have entered into it somehow. Meeting her felt like being kicked in the stomach, and I instinctively liked her from that very first meeting. To me, she glistened like a diamond in bright light, attracting me to her like a bear is drawn to honey. I suppose that statement sounds a little over the top, but that's the way she affects me. That moment turned to a defining time in my life.

When the three of us went to breakfast in Falmouth, Claire's eyes flashed a certain something I couldn't place at the time, and then it came to me. She was lonely and looking for a companion. Who better to fill the bill? You guessed it, me, of course.

Since that momentous time, my days have rested on the bright side of life. Everything happened so fast I didn't have a chance to think things over until my return to Bridgeton. After reviewing my situation, I put my mind in a hurry-up mode, and decided to go where my heart led me—to Sands Beach where Claire lives.

The truth is I've taken up with that lovely lady. I'm dazzled by her simple and striking beauty. She displays a common touch coupled with great warmth.

Charlie, my boy, you'll find this affair no common- place experience, and will have to work through it like you did in the minefields at Inchon, Korea, I thought.

My fascination with her gradually gave way to a new, but totally different encounter. Early on, I knew she was sensational, but recently discovered she had one hell of a mind.

What the hell, I thought to myself, that's no revelation to me, I knew that back in Casler. My recollection of Claire caused me to chuckle.

Going out with Claire is my idea of a good time. I even enjoy that people notice us as a couple. To be honest, I think it's because of her imposing, eye-catching visage rather than my benign, unassuming presence.

She's like a fresh breeze blowing in my direction, and possesses a subtle manner of sneaking up on me. Needless to say, that mannerism makes me feel young again. She's in a class by herself. This may be hard to believe, but Claire loves me; she told me so.

You're not the first person she told that to. I relished what went through my mind.

She displays a willingness to talk about her past, which I admire. As her history spilled out, your name came up in the conversation. She told me you weren't exciting enough, though she had a pedestrian affection for you. I wasn't surprised because you told me she walked away from you in high school.

Claire was right about me not being exciting, I thought, but I never did pass myself off as Sean Connery. I guess a pedestrian affection is better than nothing at all. My thoughts prompted me to again laugh as I returned to Charlie's letter.

You have certainly heard the expression, peel an onion and you'll find many layers. Well, that's the case with Claire. She's still carrying her share of baggage from a bad marriage, and I hear a hint of caution underlying her words. I believe her emotions run deep, but she exerts great discipline on herself to mask them.

Early on in our relationship the fact screamed at me that she was driven by an unseen demon. This may be an untenable observation, but I sense her goal from an early age was to live her life as an aristocrat, falling far short of that goal along the way. I believe there's a solution for her deep-seeded obsession, and my influence is about to change all that.

Sorry, buddy, but I'll bet you'll encounter more bumps on the road than you bargained for, I considered.

The affection I'm experiencing with Claire is not nearly the all-consuming love I had with Betty, but that's understandable, at least to me. So you see, Betty is gone but not forgotten. The discussions I had with you about my loss helped me face up to reality, and that has altered my thinking. I'm not wearing rose-colored glasses in thinking Claire is the answer to completely healing my mental scars but, nevertheless, it's been one hell of a ride so far.

As you read this message, you may be thinking romance has numerous disappointments and Claire is playing me like a bow fiddle without me realizing it. I understand there are no guarantees in life and love, but I'm not looking for guarantees. I'll risk what it takes to join the land of the living again.

For a man as worldly as him in so many aspects of aging, he is unknowingly falling short of common sense. Charlie, how clueless can you be?, I asked myself.

I can give her a life she never experienced when she married that bastard husband of hers. As far as the aristocratic style of life she strived for that I earlier alluded to, believe me, it won't happen— end of story.

We've talked at length about our relationship and arrived at some conclusions one might call guidelines. We plan on having a peaceful, controlled life that is not of the hot and cold variety. We share a fancy for vestiges of things past, a simpler time. What the hell, why not enjoy the pleasant things you grew up with?

I'm a successful and somewhat accomplished author. I believe there's a couple of novels left in this beat-up old mind. My time with Claire has been worth a king's ransom, so I've honed in on writing a love story with Claire the object of my affection.

Take care of yourself and let me know how things are with you. One last thing: Remember to keep your powder dry.

Your friend,
Charlie

Maybe a marriage to Charlie will bring Claire to her senses and a well-deserved peace. Even though I had some cynical thoughts, I'm happy for them and hope this union will bring with it a rewarding future, I reflected, while turning to the postscript of Charlie's revealing letter.

This last page may sound contrived, but believe me it is pure gospel. I finished the previous pages of this letter last night and intended to post it in the morning mail. Later in the evening something unique and exciting happened. Claire and I started talking and within an hour decided to get married, it happened that fast. Doesn't that beat all?

We're to make our home at her place on Sands Beach. My house in Bridgeton will be placed on the block and I'll become a beach bum. Well, hardly that, but you've come to know me well enough to realize this is nothing more than trash-talk. There is something I'm serious about. The wedding date is the twenty-eighth of November and the ceremony is to take place on the beach across the street from her house.

We're too old for anything fancy, just family, her kids and mine, along with our close friends. That's the way she wanted it, so she'll get her way. There will be a get-together following the wedding at a storied restaurant called The Kinsale. I got my way on this phase of the celebration and believe me when I say this will be a slam-banger reception with an expanded guest list of grand characters that will set you back a step or so.

I've neglected one important feature of this newsletter. I'd like you to be my best man and expect hearing from you shortly.

> *For the second time,*
> *Charlie*

Reflecting upon Charlie's addendum, I decided that it would take time to bring Catherine up-to-speed on attending a wedding where Claire would be the featured player. I thought it best to hold off mentioning the event until later—much later, as a matter-of-fact.

Chapter 22

The Foster family settled on the front porch at about the same time streaks of darkness appeared in the sky.

There was athletic Peggy from Charlottesville, Virginia, mother of three, women's soccer coach at the University of Virginia, and, considered by those in the family, our hard-thrower. Paul, the eldest, was a practicing dentist from Syracuse and the father of four whom I considered the diplomatic voice of reason for the Fosters. Finally, there was our baby, thirty-eight year old Donnie. A successful investment banker, he was the top wage-earner of the family. Still unmarried, he had been living with a woman for ten years, believing the arrangement was just fine the way it was.

The three sitting on the porch looked like they had been cloned. They possessed my lanky build and their mother's good looks. We sat in silence with my heart racing so fast I thought it might explode.

"I have many quality memories of our family in this house that keep bouncing around in my mind, most of which are of your mother and you kids growing up. I'm certain you know the ones I'm referring to. They are the good and not-so-good incidents that collectively make a family stronger in its later years.

"One incident comes to mind. Paul, I remember the day your mother and I were sitting on this very porch when you introduced us to a little girl you'd met on the beach. Much to our amusement you bravely announced to us that you intended marrying her." Paul appeared embarrassed while his brother and sister laughed at his discomfort.

I noticed uneasy glances passed around the porch, but pushed ahead.

"I guess we can get started. Please don't be stone-hearted about what you're about to hear. My life needs to be put in order for no other reason than time seems to be flying by for me. I'm telling you because I want you to keep a good thought of your father.

"I've been going through the motions of being busy and happy while all the time feeling lonely. My options have run out and, sadly, going it alone hasn't worked. I dare say not a day goes by that I don't think about Jane. Your mother was not only the dutiful wife and mother every man deserves, but she was my best friend and the only woman I ever loved. Oh sure, she got mad as hell at me, but that's part of the marriage deal. There's no way I can replace her nor would I attempt such foolishness. Without the words, there's no music. You kids count your blessings for having such a mother."

Peggy's eyes displayed anguished thoughts.

"With nobody but you kids to confide in, I felt as if the walls of my existence were closing in on me. Because of those thoughts, I felt it was best for you to understand my thinking rather than hearing it second-hand."

The kids glanced at each other with puzzled looks.

"I need to make a difficult decision, and your thoughts will help."

"Dad, I thought I knew how you think, but you've stumped me. Out of curiosity, where is this headed?" Paul asked.

"I'm facing a dilemma that I alone must resolve. I tried arriving at a decision based on what you kids and my close friends would say. In doing so, I lost sight of my own welfare trying to justify the end results. There's something you should know before I run out of time."

Donnie laughed. "Whoa, loosen' up, Dad, you're a long way from being over the hill."

Good old Donnie, I thought, he always sees a glass half-full, not half empty. Dismissing my notion with a shrug, the moment called for me to push ahead.

"I've met someone I knew when we were in sixth grade. We've started dating, though I don't have the deep feeling for her that came my way with your mother. Interesting enough, she appears to harbor similar feelings of love and loss for her late husband."

A broad smile crossed Donnie's face, anticipating what I was about to reveal.

"Catherine is a once-in-a-lifetime chance for me. They say that happiness follows sorrow and she appears to be my happiness. At least that's one man's opinion."

Donnie's eyes displayed a twinkle while silently puffing out his cheeks. At the same time it was becoming more apparent by the minute that my revelation had baffled the other two.

"This has nothing to do with love at first sight, far from it. I believe we have a sense of where this relationship is headed, but never discuss it."

Paul, the voice of reason asked, "Dad, have you considered this Catherine woman might like you as a friend, but not well enough to marry you?"

His practical perspective annoyed me.

"First off, I don't like the way you called her 'this Catherine woman'. Secondly, I'll cross that bridge about her feelings when I get to it. Lastly, you jumped the gun. The word marriage hasn't even been mentioned, let alone discussed." I paused to refocus. "As of now, we're just good friends." My strident voice carried a bite to it.

Sounding conflicted, Peggy's voice took on a serious tone, "Just how friendly with her are you?"

Peggy's question disappointed me, making me angry as hell, but she was my daughter and I loved her. I knew she was worried and accepted her concern.

"The only time I've touched her was on our first date when I took her by the elbow to lead her into The Boathouse restaurant on Casler Lake. You certainly must remember the restaurant." The kids nodded in agreement. "I haven't even held her hand, and that's a fact. My relationship with Catherine is like a line from an old song, 'A Fine Romance With No Kisses.'"

'Dad, you're not telling us anything. If you want the family to understand how you feel, there must be more to the story than you're revealing. It isn't fair for us to hear anything but the full story. I'll bet both Paul and Donnie agree with my thinking." Peggy's brothers nodded in agreement.

"You'll have to bear with me while I go back in time, fifty-eight years in fact."

I started my account about the sixth grade experience with Catherine, and then moved on to the Woolworth's meeting after my time in the service. I fast-forwarded the years to the present, minus any mention of Catherine. That omission was by design; she could fill in her history when she talked to the kids.

"The life she leads is of her own choosing from being a tormented young girl, through fighting her way out of a mosaic of misfortune. She's now the dignified person I met in Woolworth's, obviously much older, but the same person. Catherine is not a wallflower, nor does she have a domineering nature, she's just a nice lady who knows her mind and acts accordingly. My friend has many interests and unseen talents."

While finishing my story, Paul gave me a long look, and then followed with, "Like what?"

"For one thing, she's a volunteer at Portland Memorial Hospital. She sits with cancer victims, keeping them company while they receive chemotherapy treatment in the infusion room. Catherine spends endless hours each week at the Salvation Army clothing bazaar and food pantry. And, if that isn't enough for you, Paul, she teaches pre-school children Sunday school lessons at her church.

"She's far from a big personality with a huge ego; rather, she's a compassionate person trying to help people through a difficult time. Unlike the four of us on this porch, who haven't experienced poverty, Catherine has looked it in the eye, and understands what damage it leaves."

An awkward silence briefly reined, along with some foot shuffling, until I spoke up again.

"I'll give you another reason why I like Catherine— she gives me an inner peace much like your mother did."

Their questions upset me simply because the family meeting appeared headed in the wrong direction. Even though I knew they were asked with no malice intended; a feeling of not being able to cope with the situation swept over me.

Paul set his chin firmly. "I'd like to meet her."

"You shall, my boy. Catherine is driving down here tomorrow morning."

Displaying the hint of a smile, Donnie muttered to himself, "Well, well, well, won't the morning be an interesting event."

The conversation started to wane when Peggy stood up. "My bed is calling. Good night, family." Her tired voice set the stage for an immediate withdrawal by the others.

"Sounds like a sensible thing to do. Have a good night's rest, Dad," Paul said, following his sister into the house.

"I'm not ready for sleep. Maybe I'll grab a couple of beers at The BBC. Hang in there, Dad, and remember what you told us about the thing that follows sorrow." Donnie left the porch with a wave.

Good old, Donnie, I mused, always the optimist. Suddenly feeling emotionally drained, the thought crossed my mind that tomorrow would reveal the kid's reaction to Catherine.

Chapter 23

Saturday morning arrived too early for my taste. My kids manufactured uneasy talk while they waited at a backyard picnic table for the arrival of their father's girlfriend. I, on the other hand, sat alone, guarding against losing control of my emotions. It became apparent their nervousness was growing faster than their father's, and that was saying a lot.

My stomach turned over the moment Catherine's tan sedan pulled into the driveway. She left her car with a purpose, as if to say, 'Here I am, now make the most of it'. It was not an in-your-face gesture, but rather, 'I'm going to meet David's children on my own terms' statement.

She was the morning's centerpiece and knew it. Much to her credit, she had dressed down in casual fall attire. Tastefully dressed in a forest green short-sleeved blouse, tan walking shorts, and leather sandals, her hair was pulled back in a pony-tail and secured by a matching green ribbon. Her appearance made a distinct, confident statement.

A strange sensation settled over me as she walked toward us. Excitement melded together with apprehension settled in my thoughts. I didn't know what to expect, but what happened next proved to be an extraordinary encounter. Observing the kids' reactions from a respectable distance offered no clue as to what they were thinking.

Paul set his chin in a firm, defiant position while the shadow of doubt that covered Peggy's face could be misunderstood as suspicion. Displaying a hint of surprise, Donnie mouthed to me, "She's better looking than I figured."

I expected an awkward silence but their welcoming smiles directed at our visitor surprised me. The sincerity of their greeting wasn't clear at the moment and the change in attitude baffled me.

Catherine gave me a slight nod before turning her dignified attention to the kids. She introduced herself to my family and then talked comfortably with each of them. They gathered together with occasional sounds of laughter drifting from the group. Their response sounded encouraging.

Peggy spoke to Catherine with pursed lips. "I'd like to have a word with you."

"That would be nice."

Peggy motioned to a love seat under a nearby tree.

Once seated, Peggy asked, "Please tell me about you and Dad."

"How long have you known about us?"

"Only since last night. That's when Dad broke the news."

"What's to tell?" Catherine opened her hands.

"You know, where is this going?" Peggy's searching words appeared to unsettle my friend.

Catherine sighed while shifting her gaze to the empty beach across the street.

"Yes, I'm afraid I do." She lowered her head in confusion before shifting her brown eyes to Peggy. Time passed before she started to speak.

"Your father and I have experienced difficult times of late. Ironically, my husband and your mother passed away within months of each other three years ago. Your mother died unexpectedly while Frank, my husband, suffered a lingering illness that caused him to spiral down to a mere shadow of his former self. Watching him die broke my heart and left scars I carry to this day. I can't speak for David, but I understand his pain as you do."

Catherine's eyes misted as she prepared to lead Peggy into the gray segment of her life.

"Like your father and countless others, I'm a child of the Depression. My father lost his job on the same day I was born." A slight smile crossed her lips. "Welcome to the world, Catherine Hislop, your father is out of work. His company closed its doors because no one was buying. Although a skilled mechanic, there was absolutely no work available."

Peggy's lips made a round "O" in surprise.

"What's the first thing you remember in your life?"

Peggy appeared nonplussed, barely managing a shrug. Minutes passed before she spoke. "My first remembrance was an unusual event," her recollection caused her to smile.

"What a nice smile you have," Catherine said.

Peggy mumbled her thanks. "I was three years old when I stuck a shoehorn in an electric outlet. The shock singed the metal up to my fingers. The incident, without a doubt, captured my attention in a hurry, causing me to remember it to this day. A shocking experience if I say so myself."

They both laughed.

Paul and Donnie sat with me at the picnic table, not speaking, just passing time watching the women quietly talking and occasionally laughing. As for me, I felt saddened that I had placed my children in a position where they had to meet and judge a woman whom their father liked.

"Please tell me about the first experience you recall?" Peggy asked.

"We stayed in our home for over three years until my parents couldn't make the house payments and then we had to leave. The first thing I remember is moving to a tenant house on a farm outside a little town called Hawthorne. Dad helped the farmer by doing odd jobs to pay for the rent. We ate off the land, so to speak, until the poor farmer died. The tragedy forced us to move and that's when the real problems for my family began. We settled in a rundown shanty near the tracks in Casler during the summer before I started sixth grade. That end of town had no electric service, so we made due with kerosene lamps. Our situation improved a month later when we moved to a house with electricity. The new place was beat-up and shoddy, but better than the previous one.

"We were dirt-poor. The whole family walked the railroad tracks that ran next to our house collecting loose coal shattered along the rails. I can remember my fingers hurting from holding on to the loaded bucket handle. Mother canned whatever she could find to preserve, which wasn't much. I was always hungry, deluding myself into believing that most people grew up with empty stomachs."

Consumed by Catherine's unfolding story, Peggy's head dropped in an unabashed attitude of dismay.

"The only dress I owned was a hand-me-down from my older sister, Dorothy, that was thread-bare and aged from constant washing. My scruffy brown shoes had wear holes in the soles, with unsightly baling twine instead of shoe laces. I put cardboard in them to cover the holes. To complete my wardrobe, I claimed two holey cotton panties."

Peggy glanced teary-eyed at me with a sad look.

"I'll never forget those ugly panties—not even at this stage of my life. From the time I could afford it, I indulged myself by buying expensive lingerie with lace, always with lace. If I were to walk around in my underwear this morning, bystanders would think of me as a walking commercial for *Victoria's Secret*."

Peggy broke into uncontrolled laughter, causing Catherine to join in.

I looked at them from a distance, pleased they were getting on. My daughter was like a wild rocket that could go off at any moment, but that didn't appear to be the case this morning.

"Peggy, I'd like you to think back to when you were a twelve-year old sixth-grader starting a new school year in September. You entered your first day of school on a full stomach that never experienced hunger, and you were wearing a nice crisp dress."

Peggy nodded that she remembered.

"The September I started at Casler wasn't like that. I can remember walking to school with Dorothy, a frightened, undersized little girl wearing oversized rags. After being processed in the front office as a new student, the next thing I knew I was standing in the doorway of my sixth-grade classroom. Mrs. Warner, the teacher, was busy with another student, so I had no place to go, nothing to do but stand there and feel confused. Try to think what it would be like to be dressed like a rag doll in a strange setting, looking at kids your own age who in turn were looking back. I could hear their snide remarks and crude jokes directed at me. That abuse made me feel like running away, or certainly talking back—I did neither.

"Mrs. Warner finally came over and took the admission paper I was holding and announced, 'Class, please welcome Catherine Hislop.' Dead silence followed her announcement. She directed me to a seat next to a boy in the front row. It was at that moment David Foster entered my life. He said, 'Hi' and introduced himself. My brain shut down. I can remember feeling tongue-tied and didn't reply."

Catherine turned to smile at Peggy.

"David was nice to me. I discovered later he was one of the most popular boys in the sixth grade and when he befriended me, and somewhat acted as my protector, abuse from my classmates lessened. Oh, I was still given the cold shoulder, but I could live with that. Peggy, I remember his kindness at a time when that quality was uncommon for twelve-year-old boys."

"Catherine, Dad has always been that way, thoughtful of others. I'm not surprised he helped you through those difficult times."

"He was a God-send, but there were certain matters he couldn't help me with. When I turned twelve my body started changing. Not the usual changes a twelve–year-old girl experiences, but unsightly ones my mother couldn't account for. Large and ugly boils started appearing on my legs. Peggy, you may never have seen a boil; mine took on a shiny, distended appearance that would burst if bothered and drain yellow pus. I have no way of knowing, but I believe my poor diet coupled with the usual female changes caused the problem."

"What an unfortunate experience to have to suffer through," Peggy said with sad eyes.

Catherine laughed while extending her legs. "See, I suffered minimal damage from those nasty things. Getting back to sixth grade, learning was a pleasure for me and came easily. Mrs. Warner was an exceptional teacher who put the learning experience in a different light for me. She recognized my quick mind and went out of her way to further develop it. I experienced two events in Casler that have stayed with me. One was the sense of unbridled discovery in the classroom and the wonders of life that accompany it; the other was one I failed to recognize at the time but no less for motive. That sixth-grade experience was my first exposure to a social class pecking order. My stay in Casler was but two short months before we moved to Farmington. The move was a fresh start for me and a good job for my father after eleven years of unemployment. I learned many lessons during that brief stint in Casler, but the most memorable was one I learned from your dad—do what's right and not what's popular."

Peggy looked at Catherine with pride.

"It's my hope you can understand how coming together with your father could happen. Whether one is twelve or seventy, what's not to like about David Foster? Your father makes me feel very special."

Tears streamed down Catherine's face while surrendering to her emotions.

From the look on their faces, I sensed Peggy was well on her way to making a decision about Catherine.

"I understand now why Dad befriended you in sixth grade and why he's attracted to you now. There are many qualities about you that remind me of our mother. Here's hoping we can become good friends," Peggy said with misty eyes.

Chapter 24

After Catherine said her goodbyes and left, the Foster family gathered on the porch.

Donnie started the inevitable with, "Let the good times roll."

I think all of us realized these precious moments would provide relief from a tension-filled morning, but the absurdity of his comment caught us off guard, causing uncontrolled laughter. After the outburst, we looked at each other in an uncomfortable quiet.

Paul broke the silence. "Can we get to the point?"

"I can do that. Now that you've met Catherine, what do you think of her?"

Peggy spoke up. "Time has been kind to her."

"What do you mean by that?" I asked.

"She's young-looking with a beauty that has lasted through her years."

"That's all well and good, but there has to be more," I said.

Peggy gave me a hard look. "I'd say she's very self-assured. When we talked, she never gave an inch, and I liked that."

Being the hard-ass you are; I can see why you'd think that. I smiled at my thought.

"What are you driving at?" Donnie asked.

"Catherine's orderly mind places her life events in the appropriate order. She made me understand her teenage life had not been a bed of roses. She told her story with a great deal of warmth, not with a sign of bitterness that one would expect from someone who had. . ." Peggy stopped to take a deep breath, "I can't find a reason not to like her. That lady is special, and don't you forget it," she said with conviction.

Paul appeared conflicted before he spoke. "Catherine came off better than I anticipated, though she left a great deal to be desired."

"Scorn doesn't work for you. Shame on you anyway for talking that way," Peggy admonished.

Paul threw his hands in the air. "I wasn't being scornful or sarcastic, or whatever you want to call it, and you know it," his words carrying a sharp edge.

"Then what's your problem with her?" Peggy gravely asked.

An uneasy moment settled between bother and sister.

Paul shifted uncomfortably in his rocker. "This is a bit awkward for me, but I want to assure everyone I'm not on a witch hunt."

Peggy fixed Paul with an annoyed look. "You still haven't answered my question."

"Peggy, this isn't a one-directional discussion." He lifted his chin at me. "Dad's the centerpiece of why we're here."

"Excuse me while I go out and stand in the middle of the street and hope a car hits me. Maybe then I can get a reaction from you," Peggy replied coldly.

Paul laughed. "It's hard to believe my baby sister is such a hard case."

"You better believe it," she said belligerently, pride sweeping through her voice, "and damn proud of it."

That's my girl, I thought proudly.

"Discounting Peggy's little tantrum, I think you'll agree that everyone on this porch is exceptionally bright and understands many of life's complexities, though at times, one would never guess it." Paul glanced at Donnie who shrugged happily. "Nevertheless, we've had our say except for our resident comic. Would you care to comment, Mr. Chuckles?"

Donnie puffed out his cheeks and blew out. "I have no explanation why I like her, but I do. There's no question about it, Catherine is a winner and over the top, she's sensational!"

His voice inflection subtly changed to a serious tone. "You were lucky to meet her on time."

"On time?" I asked.

"Yes, on time. You might have hooked up with a woman unlike Catherine. You get my drift, don't you?"

I nodded in agreement but didn't answer.

"Make us happy by choosing her, and you'll be happy too," Donnie said, beaming at me.

I nervously cleared my throat. "Do you want to hear what I think?"

Paul motioned me to continue.

"Catherine's friendship has been an enormous boost to my well-being, nothing short of amazing. To provide a little perspective, allow me to read you a letter from Charlie Jamison, the writer from Virginia I talked about."

The kids nodded their approval.

I read his letter in its entirety.

"There is a parallel here between my past and the present."

I painstakingly returned the kids to Casler, describing my history with Claire from start to finish, leaving nothing out along the way. My audience appeared marginally interested in my brief account of a high school romance, but barely. They didn't react until I mentioned the junior prom debacle, and then they unleashed peals of laughter.

"The doubt that lodged in my memory bank from my experience with Claire was long-forgotten. During the many years of our married life, the thought of Jane cheating on me never crossed my mind. Seeing that I'm revealing my secrets, here's the rest. I never cheated on your mother, and I thank God I didn't.

"Since I've been seeing Catherine, the thought of infidelity surfaced, not hers mind you, but the memory of Claire's meandering ways did the trick."

I held up my hand before anyone could speak.

"I know what's on your minds. You're going to say it's childish of me to resurrect distasteful memories of so long ago, and I have to agree with you."

I sensed a feeling of impatience settling on the kids, especially a brooding Paul.

"My answer may bowl you over. What I have to say is my final decision. I have thought long and hard about this and, yes, even prayed for guidance. I gathered from Charlie's letter that he experienced not even a hint of doubt about his future relations with Claire. I wish I could say the same about my situation, but I can't. Where it came from doesn't matter, I'm saddled with doubt about moving ahead concerning matters of the heart. I think the world of Catherine and hope our friendship can remain as steadfast as it has been in the past, but I shall die as your widowed father."

Peggy didn't speak, trying vainly to control the tears that slipped down her cheeks. Donnie sported a pout I'd not seen since he was a little boy. Paul fixed me with a curious look while scratching his head.

"I'll make this simple. Dad, it's pretty obvious you've made your mind up, and that I respect, so there's little need to ask you to reconsider. I'm certain Catherine took our measure when she met us. Well, I took hers as well. In her sharp-edged manner, Peggy strongly upbraided me for not explaining my thoughts on Catherine. She even alluded to something about standing in the middle of the street to get my attention."

Donnie's pout disappeared when he broke up in laughter, while Peggy smiled through her tears.

"While Catherine and Peggy talked, for some unknown reason I thought of her being a cold, calculating woman. When she asked me to walk with her, I didn't know what to make of her request. Obviously, I agreed but strangely changed my mind about her a couple of minutes into our walk. What changed my mind you may wonder? It's hard to put a finger on it, but I think it was her kindly manner and soft melodious voice. Truthfully, I like the way she looks.

"I felt conflicted over Catherine as we walked, and tried to decide how she would take to our family. On one hand I wanted to like her because she was Dad's friend, yet the thought of her replacing Mom didn't sit well with me.

"After she took me back to when Dad was her protector in grade school, I understand the attraction they have for each other. Catherine mentioned that her husband's death left a vacancy she never filled until dad reentered her life. The depth of her bad luck left me unsettled. I haven't been around her enough to really know her, but our brief time together gave me room to experience her warmth and goodness. The reason I like Catherine is because it felt natural talking to her, and another thing; I find something about her that brings to mind our Mother. I'm a one-mother guy, but having Catherine as a friend will be just fine with me."

Silence seized the porch until Donnie spoke up.

"Our mother and father built a strong family network of which we should be proud. Granted, they did and said things that we didn't agree with, but we intuitively knew they had our best interests in mind. That's the reason we three kids get along so well."

Both Peggy and Donnie nodded in agreement.

Paul again spoke. "The three of us have known families whom we consider strong and caring. At some point in their past, I know not when, an incident occurred that fractured their well-being, forcing them to become a dysfunctional clan that never returned to its former self. The Foster family is too strong to allow that to happen. We've had our moments of discord, that's inevitable, but remember, we're Fosters because of Mom and Dad, and what they say goes.

The Foster family said their goodbyes with tears in their eyes, and hugs for all.

I sat by myself looking at the near-empty Falmouth Heights beach with a great sense of tenderness for my children, and yes, feeling lonely and sorry for myself.

The people I felt close to were no longer around. Catherine was now in New Bedford, Claire and Charlie had returned to their homes in Virginia, and the kids had left. The kids, God love them and protect them. I sensed in my heart the disappointment they felt over my feeling toward Catherine, but regardless of their sentiments, they were there for me when I most needed their love and support.

The stress-laden day finally caught up with me, causing me to drop off into a much-needed slumber. I awoke late in the afternoon with the thought—it's time to close up the beach house for good and head home for winter.

Chapter 25

The beauty of the November evening embraced us while we slowly walked along Commercial Street, fallen autumn leaves rustling under our feet. The slight mist we walked through put a sparkle on everything it touched, including us.

"The light strikes your hair in an appealing way," I suggested. Catherine managed a shrug and then smiled.

We turned into Long Wharf and headed toward DiMillo's restaurant, its lights pressed against the dark sky.

After entering the eatery, the swell of quiet conversation greeted us, along with the aroma of seafood drifting through the dining room.

"It smells wonderful in here," Catherine observed.

My interest in Catherine spiked when I looked at this gracious lady with her unpretentious ways.

Dimillo's made me feel for a fleeting instant as if I were living in a dream sequence. The scene kept nudging my memory of Jane. Back then, we came for dinner every Saturday night after a home football game, win or lose.

We were seated at a table next to a window overlooking the harbor, a small lamp lighting its surface. While looking at Catherine, my thoughts centered on how nice she looked; not beautiful, but just plain pretty. She was a well-groomed woman heading for seventy and very special to me.

I nodded toward the window. "Look at the far reaches of the harbor."

The prowl of a huge freighter was breaking through the darkness into the harbor's ambient light on its way to a familiar berthing place. The astonished look on her face told a story I didn't understand, and then it came to me. She had lived most of her adult life in Upstate Maine, and had missed such events as a large ship entering port.

"What you're enjoying is a breathtaking view of a working harbor. That's why Portland is aptly named 'The Waterfront City,' a port at its finest," I pointed out.

"I've never experienced such beauty!" Catherine's enthusiasm was captivating, reminding me of my children's excitement on Christmas morning.

Minutes passed while we silently viewed the panoramic view of a New England city preparing for winter.

"I'd like to order dinner for you if that's agreeable."

"Thank you, David, I'd like that."

"I'm treating you to an old-fashioned Down-East dinner. It's called Bouillabaisse and is of French origin."

Catherine appeared uncertain about my choice of a main course. "I've heard of it, but know little about the dish."

"It's a thick soup consisting mainly of shellfish such as shrimp, oysters, clams, and mussels, plus a variety of white fish served over toasted French bread. There's more to it than I know, but you'll love it."

After serving drinks, the waitress took our dinner orders.

On an impulse, I waved my hand in a sweep of the harbor. "Your beauty exceeds this magical setting."

Catherine made a flustered smile. "You continually embarrass me with your nutty talk."

"I didn't mean for that to happen, but sometimes dumb words slip out when I don't know what else to say."

A roving violinist stopped at our table favoring us with a treasured song from the late forties, "I'll Be With You In Apple Blossom Time." Hearing that tune caused me to retreat into a mini daydream that focused on Claire Franklin. That was our song during the brief time we dated.

I thought of three women who by varying degrees impacted my life.

My fleeting time with Claire Franklin was a high school romance more aptly called an encounter with infatuation. The minimal time I knew Catherine Hislop could be considered nothing more than puppy love. After all, I was only twelve at the time and didn't understand such things as love. On the other hand, Jane taught me the true meaning of love. Now I find myself sitting across the table from a much more mature version of my earlier puppy love.

"We need to talk," I said with urgency.

"We are," she said with a smile.

"This is different though. There are matters between us that need to be discussed," I explained.

She directed an understanding smile at me. "I know the feeling."

"The attraction I have for you didn't start overnight, far from it. Every time I think back to sixth grade in Casler, images of a sad little girl sitting next to me come to mind."

Catherine's eyes filled with the distant memory of that depressing time, brought more immediate and vivid through her tears.

"We are living with the discipline of time looking over our shoulders. The days have turned to months since we became reacquainted with one another. In the beginning, I felt awkward and had trouble sorting out my thoughts."

I could sense my voice faltering, but pushed ahead.

"I learned a great deal from you when we were twelve, but you probably didn't realize it at the time."

Catherine's puzzled look caused me to laugh.

"Now that we're seventy, I'm still learning from you. Your zest for life has rubbed off on me, and the subtle touch you display in all matters has given me something to hold on to."

Silence again claimed the table. Words I wanted to say finally came to mind.

"When we're together, I'm happy and I yearn to be with you when I'm not."

"David, we can't reinvent the past to suit our current situation no matter how much you wish to. It can never be the same."

She looked away, taking time to taste her wine.

"Let's face it, over the last several years, we've experienced difficult times." The start of a smile settled on her face. "Are you thinking of us in a more permanent connection? If you are, your thoughts sound like a normalcy we both desperately seek, yet find unattainable."

Catherine's gentle rebuke caused me to gaze into the distance. Jane, my lifelong love, pushed into my thoughts. She possessed insight accompanied by an enviable practicality that I took for granted. The fact finally sunk in that Catherine claimed many of those same qualities.

I exhaled deeply, telling myself I started this conversation, but had lost track of where it was heading.

"Aren't you forgetting someone?"

Her voice snapped me out of reverie.

"Sorry, I was having a little conversation with myself."

She sighed but made no comment.

"Catherine, every time I'm happy, you come to mind."

"The manner in which we have revisited an earlier friendship has been enchanting. I'm pleased you're happy when we're together, but can there be more for us?" Catherine asked.

"Our magical encounter, if one chooses to call it that, didn't occur by chance." I glanced skyward. "What happened was written on the stars, and you know it."

She captured the moment with her smile. "David Foster, you're a good man with whom I love spending time. Maybe we should begin our salads."

We followed her suggestion by starting our salads, not talking, just eating.

The nagging thought that our relationship wasn't working the way I wanted wouldn't go away. Anything is possible, I dubiously thought, but am I ready to make a commitment, or is she, for that matter?

An inner voice spoke to me: "Dave Foster, face the truth. Your ability to reason vanishes when Claire enters your thoughts. Forget the hope you're harboring that she'll end up with you; Claire is spoken for. Charlie will soon marry her, leaving you out in the cold looking in. Your favorable memory of her has no rational basis. You never got along with Claire until after she dumped you. That alone speaks volumes. You never did love her nor do you now.

"And there's Catherine. One moment you're telling her about something written on the stars, minutes later, you're asking yourself whether making a commitment to her is in your best interest. You passed over the obvious with the vacillating attitude you've displayed toward her. Do the right thing for yourself and get rid of those thoughts concerning the past. Catherine is the woman for you; so, the sooner you accept that fact, the happier you'll be."

After finishing our salad, I reminded myself that there was more to this dinner than fine food. The time was right to spring Charlie's letter on her.

"You've heard me talk about Charlie Jamison, the author from Virginia. I received a letter from him the other day and I'd like you to read it."

After finishing Charlie's correspondence, Catherine sighed yet made no comment, apparently lost in her own thoughts. One glance explained her thinking—she was not happy. Something in the letter must have set her off.

Chapter 26

Catherine's eyes settled on me with a bristling glare. Shaking her head, she announced, "I'm not going with you!" Her voice rife with meaning had taken on a bitter cast.

Uneasy thoughts flashed by me once her words registered.

"It's something I don't want to do alone," I informed her. "Can you be persuaded to change your mind?"

Exasperation covered her flushed face. "Something unpleasant between us will happen if I go. Believe me, I know what you're thinking and it will be the same old story. Certain things in life don't change and she's one of them."

I had an inkling of what she meant, but wanted to hear her say it.

"You're talking about Claire?" I asked.

She nodded her head. "You can say that, and while we're at it, let me make my feelings clear about that woman. Hate is like bad weather, it's always around—at least it is with me."

Her intense eyes welled up, threatening to overflow with tears.

"That doesn't help me understand your loathing for Claire. What evidence do you have that warrants this harsh feeling?"

"I don't need evidence to justify my thoughts. By the way, what is your interest in Claire?" Catherine doggedly asked.

"She's an old friend, nothing more. As you well know, we all live with past mistakes and I'm certain Claire is no exception."

"Claire is not a nice person and has little use for me. She's one of a kind and you know it!" Catherine spoke sharply.

"You don't know that."

"David, I know what I know and Claire Franklin is a callous, unpleasant woman. A leopard doesn't change its spots!"

"There's something you overlooked. Your unpleasant moments with Claire happened many years ago."

"If you only knew what's on my mind, you wouldn't be so cavalier about my attitude. The last time I saw her wasn't long enough for me!"

Catherine seemed aggravated to the point where I thought she'd walk away from me. She didn't make a move to leave, but just sat there starring blankly ahead. Our table suddenly felt like the only one in the restaurant that was silent.

"Please forgive me for upsetting you so. Your thoughts about Claire are obviously warranted and, you have every right to feel the way you do."

"Thank you for considering my feelings but you must understand where this revulsion for her came from."

Afraid of saying something stupid that would send her over the edge, I chose not to speak.

"Do you remember the day she embarrassed me in gym class?" her intense eyes willed me to answer. I knew instinctively she was replaying the scene in her head.

My mind rushed down memory lane to Mr. Gould's square-dancing class. The image of Catherine racing from the gym in tears caused me to grimace.

"I do. It is not a nice memory," I said, heartsick from remembering.

Catherine spoke through tears. "I've been thinking about that gym class from the time I started climbing out of the ashes of despair and now you want me to give her a pass on what she did?"

Her argument is more practical than mine, I thought.

"There is one more thing," she said forcefully, "memories of Claire Franklin hurt like an arrow in my heart."

Maybe we can work this out, I thought, but it's important she knows where I stand.

"There's something you need to know. I'm not going to get down on my knees and grovel about this wedding matter."

"That's your decision, not mine," she quickly answered.

Here was a collision of wills, exerted by two people with different opinions, sitting respectively at a high-end Portland restaurant. Very civilized, I thought, but I must change the mood of this conversation.

"Let me explain my reasoning. We could have the time of our lives down there." I put the thought out ever so gently. "Here's a plan you might like. How about doing the rounds in DC, followed by some time in Charlottesville? You know, touring the University of Virginia campus and Monticello. We could slip over for the wedding and be out of there before hardly anyone noticed."

The hint of a smile settled around her eyes. "It does sound tempting."

I waited for the question that would eventually come and finally did.

"What can I expect?"

"Warmer weather than we're accustomed to up here."

Her smile turned warm and full. "I know that, silly, but there must be more to it than that."

How can I deny her anything with such a smile? I asked myself.

"There is. We'd be with each other for an extended period of time and get to really know each other. By that I mean learning about our likes and dislikes in foods, entertainment, sight-seeing favorites and other activities that don't come to mind at the moment."

"You mentioned this trip to Virginia and the wedding affair too quickly for me to assimilate. I need time to think about it."

Minutes passed while she unseeingly looked at the harbor.

"Do you think this is an easy decision for me?"

"No, I don't. But knowing is better than not knowing."

"And what should I know?"

"Attending the wedding is a small price to pay for the nice time we'll have together. You'll have to make the most of any unpleasant situations that may arise between you and Claire, though I doubt there will be any. I'm not saying it will be easy, it won't, but you're thick-skinned and tough, much more so than Claire, believe me."

She gave me a slight nod while color rose in her cheeks. I felt she liked my compliment.

Catherine seemed well on her way to coming around to my way of thinking, but remained silent.

The glint in her eyes indicated I had guessed right.

"It's your call, you've convinced me," she said with a brilliant smile.

Moments passed while I pondered Catherine's reaction. Why the dramatic shift in her attitude concerning the wedding? Maybe the trip appealed to her more than the thought of meeting Claire, I speculated.

"There you go!" I said eagerly. "You're a peach."

"Thank you for saying that, but there's something else."

Here we go again. I wonder what she has in mind.

"What is the something else you mentioned?" I asked, having no idea where she was heading.

"As I see it, minor decisions between us have been resolved but what about the major one?"

Her line of questioning puzzled me. "The major one?"

"Yes, the major one."

It appeared she had set the ground rules for my southern junket. While reflecting on her query, my vacant look prompted her to speak.

"I'm not a starry-eyed youth with Pollyanna thoughts of right and wrong. Nevertheless, this fact should stand alone. I will not besmirch Frank's memory by sharing your bed," she stated emphatically.

"Whatever you say is fine with me," I reluctantly capitulated to her wishes.

"In that case, there will be one room for me and one room for you," she happily declared.

"Does that mean all roads lead to Sands Beach?" I asked.

"Indeed."

At that moment our waitress delivered two large bowls of incredible bouillabaisse, loaded with pieces of fish and a variety of shellfish.

Chapter 27

I pulled into The Kinsale's parking lot, one of the first arrivals. The eight-mile drive from Scots Harbor to Sands Beach passed through dazzling colors that accompany a Virginia fall.

The breathtaking view from our vantage point was even more spectacular than Claire had portrayed it. A long strip of white sand, an elevated macadam walkway four feet higher than the beach, and then a grass belt between it and the street filled the snapshot view.

We stood for minutes studying the simple panoramic scene playing out in front of us. Catherine finally spoke. "The beach is so frail and vulnerable, while Maine's coastline is so formidable and unapproachable."

"Spoken like a true college professor," I smiled.

"I was a librarian, not a teacher. You know that," she said while flipping her hair.

A flock of squawking seagulls passed overhead preparing to land on the beach. The noise they emitted momentarily disrupted our thoughts.

"The pristine beauty of this beach is stunning," she said in an excited voice.

We started walking toward the place Charlie would marry Claire. By the time we settled at the wedding site, I noticed several men sneaking a look at Catherine and didn't like it.

Looking off in the distance, Catherine's thoughts seemed to be elsewhere. Returning to the present, she observed, "This is a totally new experience for me. I'll remember it for the rest of my life." She smiled at me shyly.

The start of the wedding was upon me when a person I didn't know motioned me to take my place. I left Catherine to walk down four steps to the beach where an eight-by-eight brown carpet had been placed on the sand. I took my position next to

Charlie at the back of the makeshift altar, a pot of flowers on each side.

He appeared uncomfortable while rubbing his mouth. "Do you have the ring?"

I nodded. It became apparent with each passing second that he was a nervous wreck.

"This is worse than having the Koreans shooting at me."

"Relax, Charlie; just calm down," I counseled.

"Yeah, right!" he said while on the way to becoming completely undone.

I glanced at a bright-eyed and composed Claire on her son Bobbie's arm, slowly walking toward us. She was elegantly dressed in a high-end light brown suit with burnt orange adornments, tears beginning to form in her eyes.

I whispered to Charlie. "How would you like a nice cold glass of beer on this special day?"

He didn't appreciate my humor. "Why are you talking so crazy? I have more on my mind than beer."

Claire, on Bobbie's arm, moved next to Charlie.

At the appointed hour of two o'clock, the minister motioned the wedding party to step forward, the warm Virginia breeze gently embracing us. In an impeccable Southern drawl, the man of God brought a plain Protestant wedding ceremony, lacking the traditional bells and whistles, underway.

Suddenly, brilliant colors of the rainbow captured everyone's attention. A clear sky without an indication of rain puzzled all who watched. This was an apparition created only by God for the couple standing next to me, or so I thought.

The minister seized the moment, bringing up God's power that had blessed this union.

The double-ring ceremony moved along, followed by the vows.

Claire recited her pledge in a slow, confident voice loud enough for the fifty or so guests standing on the walkway above her to hear. Charlie, on the other hand, performed in a bungling, error-laden manner.

After pronouncing them man and wife, the minister turned to the guests. "Friends, it is my pleasure to present, Mr. and Mrs. Charles Jamison."

After applause drifted down from the assembled guests, a gentle smile shown on Claire's lips, while Charlie blew out his cheeks and sighed in a show of relief.

The newlyweds moved to the macadam walk to receive greetings and congratulations from their guests. They shook hands and hugged each guest, taking more time with some than others. Catherine and I took a place at the end of the line, patiently waiting our turn.

I looked at a smiling Charlie Jamison. My recollection of him started on a Cape Cod beach when he was fighting through an advanced stage of depression. Now, four months later, here I stand on a Virginia beach waiting in line to congratulate him on getting married.

"I'll stand behind you." Catherine moved her hand forward in a sweeping 'go ahead' motion. "You know them, I don't."

The inner recesses of my mind warned me to expect Catherine to create a scene when greeting Claire. I dismissed that thought as being an old man's worry.

"As usual, love and decorum capture the day at a wedding," I said with pride, thinking my observation rather clever.

Catherine gave me a tender, approving look. "Weddings are nice, aren't they?"

"Depends on whose wedding it is. I'd like it a lot more if it were ours." I smiled over a shrug.

She ran her eyes over me with an indication of approval.

As the line moved forward, she spoke softly so no others would hear. "I dread the thought of meeting her."

"Ah, Claire's not a bad sort."

The hard look leveled at me indicated she was unhappy with my assessment. "Claire is masquerading as something she's not!"

It seemed my nerve endings were fighting to jump through my skin. The fact finally sunk in —this was not going to be a pleasant day for me.

Moving closer to the happy couple, Catherine gave the smiling bride a long glance, and then pointed out, "She doesn't look her age."

"Nor do you," I whispered.

Quickly approaching the happy couple, I focused on Claire. You have come of age, I happily thought. Enjoy your day, you deserve it. You and I have breached the divide we once knew into a new kind of friendship.

The moment had arrived, our turn was next.

"I feel so uncomfortable," Catherine whispered.

"You're doing just fine."

I stepped forward. "It's good to see you again, Claire. You've done well for a kid from Casler. Congratulations on marrying this handsome man."

Charlie was all smiles. "I like the way you talk, my friend."

She gave me a hearty kiss, and then responded with her million-dollar smile, followed by a rousing laugh that only she could produce.

"I'm pleased you think so," she said while tapping Charlie on the arm.

"Claire, I'd like you to meet Catherine Cooper."

Catherine offered her hand with a half-hearted handshake. A model of propriety, she moistened her lips, preparing to speak.

"Hello, congratulations on your wedding."

"I know you from some place, don't I?"

Catherine answered with a generic response. "My face draws that kind of reaction."

After the formality of wishing them well, we walked away.

Catherine accurately observed, "She didn't remember who I am! Can you believe it?"

Walking on, an urge to check out the newlyweds seized me. I was amazed by what I saw. Claire's lips were making a round "O". She had made the connection of the woman accompanying me, to the Catherine Hislop of Casler, Maine.

Chapter 28

We took our time while the other guests hustled toward The Kinsale. Sands Beach presented a new experience for us, so why not take advantage of it? Finally reaching the fancy restaurant, we headed for the basketball court-sized patio where a full-blown cocktail party was well underway. Those in attendance had their priorities firmly in place causing a three-deep crowd at the patio bar.

One glance at the crowd spoke volumes—this was not a stationary event where guests nestled in one spot and left it at that; much like water, they chose to mill around and sought their own level of pleasure. Charlie and Claire's patio reception was turning into the slam-banger he had promised.

After a frantic ten minutes, I returned to Catherine with our drinks, a white wine in a glass for her and a pint of beer in a plastic cup for me. She thanked me with a nod.

After a quick survey of the gathering, I laughingly asked, "Isn't this something?"

She smiled in agreement.

Guests displayed a broad selection of dress. Some wore designer clothes, others in casual attire. Whatever they wore made little difference; they were here for a party and planned to make the most of it. They smiled a lot, laughed even more, and drank all they could get their hands on, all the while moving every which way around the covered porch. I spotted several genuine characters probably responsible for providing source information for one of Charlie's novels. We had come upon and joined a senior extravaganza.

We walked to the beach side of the patio to avoid the party traffic. Catherine's eyes swept the beach, totally covered with white sand.

"My word!" she exclaimed.

"Claire called it a gift from the gods," I recalled.

Catherine's expression turned to a scowl. "This time of year, the beach was bathed in a different light, casting a golden aura on the ceremony."

She inhaled deeply. "I know. Have you noticed the smell of salt in the air is stronger than at the beach?"

I mumbled a "yes", more interested in studying the crescent-shaped beach than talking about salt smell in the air. While white-caps topped gently-breaking waves on their way to kissing the sand, the descending sun created distorted shadows, causing the water to sparkle. A handful of beach lovers walked in the silent surf, playfully splashing each other.

Seemingly lost in thought time passed while we stood in silence. There was little need for words.

"It's hard to turn your head on a setting like this. I'm dazzled by the simple beauty of Sands Beach," Catherine observed.

"I'd call it fall on the fly in Virginia," I said.

"I know Virginia is considered a southern state, but the colors down here are much like the ones back home."

I smiled at Catherine. "Your eye for beauty continually amazes me."

The man in charge of the wedding ceremony accompanied by Claire's matron of honor approached us. He offered his hand and smiled. "Hello, we meet again. I'm Jack O'Brennan and this is my wife, Jeanette."

"It's good to meet you, Jack, and you, Jeanette. I'm Dave Foster, and this is Catherine Cooper."

"I know who you are. Your Potham team played us, Elon that is, in the eastern playoffs. That team of yours beat us like a drum."

Thinking of the game O'Brennan referenced caused a broad smile to cover my face.

"I remember that game. After the Elon win, we went on to capture the National Division III Championship."

Catherine and Jeanette, appearing deep in a quiet conversation, finally drifted off to join the high-octane, churning revelers.

"And I know about you, Jack. Charlie told me he had patterned the central figures in several of his novels after you."

He laughed. "Secrets never stay secrets very long."

We talked for several minutes about football, and then he drifted off.

My kind of guy, I thought.

The level of chatter and nonsensical laughter grew with each minute that ticked by when I noticed Catherine talking to a red-headed stranger. Taller than she, he looked down at her and smiled. Whatever he said must have caught her fancy, causing her to smile and laugh outrageously.

The green monster of jealousy reached in and unceremoniously grabbed my mind, prompting thoughts I was not familiar with. Seeing her in that situation infuriated me to no end, causing a complete loss of reasoning. I could hear Charlie talking, but his words didn't register. The only thought on my mind was walking over to the stranger and punching him in the mouth for talking to Catherine.

"What right does that guy have carrying on a conversation with her like a schoolboy? What is he, a lothario or what?" I spoke softly to myself.

I started walking toward the two, fully intent on following up on my intentions of punching him out when a voice in my head spoke, stopping me in my tracks.

"Why are you so exercised over Catherine talking to that man?" The voice asked. "After all, they're only talking. A moment ago, thoughts of never experiencing what you now feel crossed your mind. Think back to Casler. You were going with Claire Franklin when Dick Thorton entered the scene. Do you remember him? He was the kid from Portland who lived with his grandparents at their cottage on Casler Lake during the summer.

"You saw him sitting on a bench in front of Richardson's drug store with Claire. The very sight of them drove you crazy, but you never mentioned your feelings to her. What you experienced back then was a justifiable case of jealousy. Now you're jealous again for no good reason.

"Claire toyed with the opposite sex just for fun, while using her good looks and personality to string guys along like you, David Foster. You knew she had a wandering eye, but overlooked her frailties because you were so enraptured with her. You placed those unpleasant truths about her in your subconscious for safe keeping.

"On the other hand, you know in your heart that Catherine isn't that way. Her DNA speaks volumes about the kind of woman she is and the person you've grown to love, though you won't admit it. Do yourself a favor and wipe out that junk about the past, and allow your heart to lead you to a new and happy life."

I snapped out of my reverie, thinking I had experienced the same thought when Catherine and I had dinner at Dimillo's.

I turned and headed toward Charlie, disregarding the blueprint I had mapped out for the unknown intruder. My mind raced back to the eventful Saturday I told the kids my relations with Catherine couldn't go any further than a close relationship. I had elusive doubts about moving on with her, or any one else, for that matter.

Still shaken from my thoughts, I joined Charlie. He pointed to an empty spot of pavement. "Why were you standing over there by yourself?"

"Just thinking," I absently replied.

"It must have been earth-shattering. You spent a bunch of time doing it."

I was in no mood to carry on a long-winded conversation with him, thus my crisp answer, "It was."

Disregarding my brusque answer, Charlie proceeded to point out some of his eccentric friends when Catherine approached.

Catherine approached us with a smile. "Charlie, I just talked to one of your friends, a fellow named Red Ted. He is truly a character."

Charlie smiled. "Red is at least that, and maybe a little more."

"He told me some wonderful stories about your writing career, but the one about Jeanette O'Brennan's restaurant burning down is the best."

"Go ahead, Catherine, let's hear what Red had to say," Charlie suggested

Catherine smiled. "I'd love to. It seems before Jack O'Brennan married Jeanette, she owned The Red Leather, a fashionable restaurant in Bridgeton. Jack was investigating a gang killing at the time when someone torched the restaurant to retaliate against him." Catherine smiled. "In one of his lighter moments, that's how Red described it; just for laughs, Jack inferred to a fire investigator that he believed Charlie Jamison might be the culprit so he could experience a building burning down, which he would later use in a novel he was writing."

The improbable story Catherine relayed caused me to laugh.

Charlie interrupted. "Let me finish this up."

She laughed, and then said with a sweep of her hand, "Be my guest."

"Between the police officers and fire investigator, they put yours truly in jail, grilling me to no end. Even after claiming my innocence, the bastards were going to give me a lie detector test. Fortunately for me, I could prove being in Atlanta at the time of the fire, or I'd have ended up in the can until O'Brennan would have jumped in and saved my sorry butt."

Chapter 29

After making the rounds of talking and joking with guests, the happy couple finally joined us. Several minutes of strained conversation followed before Claire startled me with her request.

"Catherine, could we talk?"

She replied with a straight-lipped nod.

Claire led the way to an empty spot.

I asked Charlie, "What's that all about?"

His shrug answered my question.

"From the time you passed through the receiving line, a voice in my head told me I couldn't rest until I talked to you. This effort is meant to make amends for not recognizing you and, more than that, for times that would best be forgotten, but aren't. Call this a confessional if you wish, but I must forge ahead."

"You appear to be sincere, but what is it you want from me?" Catherine asked, displaying her tenacious side.

"I went through school detached and unflappable, occasionally saying mean words, and treating others badly from the time I can remember." Claire bit down on her lip in a nervous gesture. "As I look back, the memory of you receiving so much of my hostility saddens me, especially at a time when you were so vulnerable and couldn't defend yourself. Fortunately, you had a classmate named Dave Foster who befriended you and softened my vindictive words and actions. I sometimes wondered how you survived it."

"I lived with pride in myself; it's what got me through my brief stay in Casler. I still wear it as a badge of honor, it's a Hislop trait."

"Nevertheless, it took great courage to come down here with Dave, knowing I was involved."

"No, it isn't that way. Don't think I haven't enjoyed your wedding, because I have."

"How could you be so strong?"

"The good Lord has blessed me. First, I had a loving family who taught me how to fight through adversity. I met and married a man whom I loved, and was good to me and my children. Several years ago, I lost Frank. His absence was devastating, but I managed to push through my sadness. Then came David. He has made a huge difference in my life. My strength came from all of the above. What about you, Claire, you must have some hidden thoughts about the route your life has taken?"

Charlie interrupted the ladies' conversation when he served them fresh drinks. Claire picked up the conversation after he left.

"I was the brightest of the bright in elementary school until you came along, and then I became second best. I instinctively disliked you for that, and acted accordingly."

Claire sipped her wine and then moved to a different standing position.

"One could call me snobbish, yet friendly, if that makes any sense. I was a teenager living two extremes. My father's success with the hardware store provided me a unique status among my friends. My clothes were nicer, I always bought in the school cafeteria, and I had Dad's nice car to drive around. I got along well with the other kids, was popular, I guess, but there was something else I couldn't account for."

Claire grimaced, and then pointed to a collection of unoccupied chairs close at hand.

"My feet are killing me." Once seated, Claire took her shoes off with a sigh. "There, that's better. I should be wearing sensible shoes but no, I'm nothing but a crazy old woman trying to act young by wearing those ridiculous heels, and my feet are telling me it isn't working."

Claire's laugh was loud enough to cause the guests to turn and smile.

Claire has the best laugh I've ever heard a woman make, Catherine told herself. I like her for the frailty she's not afraid of showing.

"I'll finish this up so we can get back to the party. I sometimes had bad moments when a dark spell surfaced, causing me to dislike myself later. I wasn't a nice person for those actions. I'm being uncharitable to myself you may think, but I mean it."

Claire paused to make a disheartened sigh.

"This has nothing to do with how I treated you back in Casler, but it's important that you understand why my marriage to Charlie means so much to me. My marriage was an unhappy helter-skelter ordeal. It produced good kids whom I'm proud of, the only true success in my life.

"The bigger picture came when I met Charlie at Falmouth Heights. I was a tormented woman who turned her life around with a simple wedding ceremony."

"What I'm hearing is way beyond what I expected from you," Catherine admitted.

"I know, but it just slipped out, and I feel better for saying it. There's something else that needs saying. The memory of what I did to you can't be eliminated, but please forgive me for the way I treated you when we were kids. I'd also like to be your friend."

"Claire Jamison, my mind has a built-in eraser that can instantly be activated. I just put it in motion; now you have a friend for life, count on it."

The two women hugged each other, relieved to have addressed and moved beyond the past.

Claire laughed heartily. "I think we should get back to the men standing over there." She pointed to Charlie and me.

"You mean the man you just married and my future husband, David, although he doesn't know it yet?"

Claire's million-dollar laugh could be heard around the patio as they walked hand-in-hand toward us.

I can't believe what I'm seeing, crossed my mind.

"Let's go Charlie, we have more people to see." Claire winked at Catherine as if to say, "You can see who the boss is."

Watching them leave, I turned to Catherine.

"I'll tell you about it later." She had read my mind.

Dusk was falling with startling speed.

At that moment, I realized there wasn't a single doubt in my mind about a future with Catherine and intended to move to a happy ending, sooner rather than later—if she'd have me.

She noticed my eyes when reaching to hold her skirt down. I had been caught in the act of sneaking a peak when a sudden breeze toyed with her flared garment.

Excitement rising in her eyes, she asked with a mischievous smile, "May I ask what you have in mind?"

"The race belongs to the swift." My foolish answer didn't fit the question, but caused her contented face to break out in a broad smile.

The wedding gathering slowly drifted inside for dinner as darkness approached.

I reached for Catherine's hand, her touch sealing an unspoken covenant. At that time, our quiet conversation took on a different dimension.

"What do you think our chances are?" Catherine softly murmured.

I gave her a puzzled look.

"I'm not sure what you mean," I foolishly said.

"You know, is there time for us? Is love enough?"

"The good Lord willing, we'll make time when we get home."

Catherine smiled with eyes beginning to tear. "I shall remember what you just said for the rest of my life."

"I can't love you any more than I do at this moment," I said with feeling.

She remained silent, savoring what, to this point, had only been hoped for and now expressed with feeling.

Her eyes dancing, Catherine said with a confident voice, "David Foster, there's a place in my heart for you. To repeat what I just heard, I can't love you any more than I do at this moment."

We joined together in a kiss that reflected our need to be as one.

"David, I've kissed you before, but you've never kissed me until now."

I laughed. "What the hell, the kiss you're so proud of happened fifty-eight years ago."

Catherine's face held a gigantic smile. "I heard this line in a movie whose title escapes me, but with a slight modification, it serves the purpose. A kiss is still a kiss regardless of when it happened."

"Our first kiss since 1942," I said proudly.

"And not our last; that, you can depend on."

"We have to start someplace," I haltingly suggested.

"Bring your luggage to my room, we'll start there," she replied.

"We're finally together."

She again offered an extraordinary smile. "You can bank on it, and just to let you know, I wouldn't have it any other way."

I smiled all over. "It's taken me fifty-eight years to get you into bed."

"A pleasant way to start our years together," Catherine said, her eyes bright and shiny.

Swelled with success, her answer left little doubt what my future would bring.

About the Author

Ed Matthews lives with his wife, Carol, in upstate New York's Greater Rochester area. A graduate of Alfred University, he was employed as a history teacher and football coach at Caledonia-Mumford Central School for thirty-two years. He is a veteran of the Korean War and served two terms as mayor of the Village of Caledonia. Ed is the father of four grown children and nine grandchildren. *Bench Talk* is his sixth published effort.

ALSO AVAILABLE FROM SQUARE CIRCLE PRESS

Cornflower's Ghost

An Historical Mystery

Thomas Pullyblank

ISBN-13: 978-0-9789066-5-8
ISBN-10: 0-9789066-5-9
LCCN: 2009934094
SCP Product #: SCP-0016
Retail Price: $19.95
Physical: 232 pages; softcover

"... a vastly entertaining novel ... that pulls you in and keeps you thinking long after you've turned the last page."

Brian Carso Jr., Misericordia University

"... a vivid reminder that the past is always with us, and it profoundly affects how we live in the present and how we shape the future."

Paul D'Ambrosio, New York State Historical Association

Thomas Pullyblank has skillfully woven a tapestry of historical mystery and modern-day campus politics into a uniquely American story that addresses the larger question of how our past should or should not be employed to address contemporary issues. Based upon two hundred years of upstate New York history, **Cornflower's Ghost** translates meticulous research into believable historical characters and events. As with the lessons of history, each of the contemporary characters strives not just to solve a historical puzzle, but rather to gain some degree of self-understanding.

FOR MORE INFORMATION VISIT WWW.SQUARECIRCLEPRESS.COM

www.ingramcontent.com/pod-product-compliance
Lightning Source LLC
Chambersburg PA
CBHW030531020726
47494CB00004B/1312